DASH ALLMAN, PI, VOLUME 1

Copyright © Diane Bator, 2024

Published by Escape With a Writer Publishing

Print ISBN: 978-1-7383328-4-7

Digital ISBN: 978-1-7383328-5-4

Cover by Diane Bator

All rights reserved. Except for use in any review, the reproduction or utilization of this work in whole or in part in any form by any electronic, mechanical, or other means, now know of hereafter inserted, including xerography, photocopying, and recording, or in any information storage or retrieval system is forbidden without the written permission of the publisher.

The author prohibits any entity from using the publication for purposes of training artificial intelligence (AI) technologies to generate text, including without limitation technologies that are capable of generating works in the same style or genre as this publication. The author reserves all rights to license uses of this work for generative AI training and development of machine learning languages models.

All characters and situations in this book are fictional and have no relation whatsoever to anyone bearing the same name or names.

Dedication

Matt, Will & Athena – You are my heart and soul! Love you forever and always!

My mom, Trudy, for life and love. You're going to need a bigger bookcase.

Darryl & Kathy for road trips, long talks, and never ending support and encouragement. Oh, and see above...

My dear friend and confidante, Jay. Thanks for the many pep talks and kicks in the butt.

Mickey Mikkelson at Creative Edge Publicity, thanks for introducing me to the most amazing people and getting word out.

To everyone who has been a part of my journey – then and now – Thank You!

Follow your passions and live the life you love.

· ♥ · ♥ · ♥ · ♥ · ♥ ·

Contents

Introduction — VI

Once Upon a Crime

On Beach Time

Son of a Witch

Visions of Gumdrop

The Cat Lady's Secret

Jokers Wild

Gone to the Dolls

About the Author — 213

Also from Diane Bator — 214

Introduction

A Tribute to the late Jimmy Buffett

I was struggling with what to write this month. Personally, things have been a bit crazy, hectic, weird, wonky, whatever over the past three months. Then Jimmy Buffett died September 1, ironically at the end of summer when school returns and life resumes as normal (even thought it's technically still summer until the Fall Equinox on September 23). Normally, I wouldn't do a tribute or anything to anyone but Jimmy has held a special place in my heart the past three months. You see, I've been listening to his music every day all day long since I moved! No idea why. But it helped me through a lot of the hard stuff.

Jimmy even made his way into a short story I wrote and published: My phone fell off the table while Jimmy Buffett serenaded me about looking for salt over my earbuds.

In fact, the main character of that story will appear in future ones. So will Jimmy.

It wasn't only his love of the sea and his storytelling that I enjoyed, but how he lived life to the fullest and got to do what he loved best. Is that my takeaway from the past three months?

What I love to do the most is to write. To create. To tell stories. To take time to rest and relax in between all the big stuff. A-HA! There's my treasure! I've been one of those people who has juggled so much for so long that relaxing is difficult. I still have to be busy.

A friend called one day and I told her I was being lazy. My version of lazy was editing a book! Her version was sitting and enjoying a cup of coffee. It was a weird moment when I realized I've been so trained to constantly do and have never taken a lot of time to just enjoy the fruits of my labor. To celebrate the new books. To savor the reviews and the comments. To treat myself when I reach the milestones: finished books, published books, moving across the country to a new life.

There will always be deadlines. Always be another book, more podcasts, work to do, and dramas to smooth over - mostly not mine!

That short story I mentioned? It's called On Beach Time. While the main character, Dash, is a private detective, she takes life one case at a time while listening to Jimmy Buffett songs. It was also the most fun I've had writing in years! And she will be back!

I have been told recently that I work too hard. I take on too much. I need to play more. It's all true. This fall, I'm working on finding balance in my life and time to do the things I love!

Is that what you've been trying to tell me all summer, Jimmy?

Keep your toes in the sand,

Diane Bator

September 2023

ONCE UPON A CRIME

DIANE BATOR
DASH ALLMAN MYSTERY, BOOK 1

Once Upon a Crime

Dash Allman PI, Book 1

Diane Bator

Escape With a Writer Publishing

Once upon a time, there was a girl named after a handsome mystery writer her mom was in love with. Dashiell Hammett. Deep down, I think she wanted her daughter to become a famous mystery writer. Or a nurse. Or a lawyer.

Oh, boy, was she disappointed!

After much foot-stomping and humiliation – as well as at least one fist fight a year in school – the girl shortened her name to Dash. It was the only name change her mother would consent to until she was an adult and could legally become someone else.

By then, Dash had stuck. Although deep in the girl's heart, she longed to be named Sofia or Julie, anything but Dash.

Okay. It was me. I'm Dash.

Although my mother still calls me Dashiell Agatha Allman. Go ahead and laugh. Everyone else does. Currently, I'm a private detective-slash-beach bum. I'm not a mystery writer, or a lawyer, but I see the nurses at the local hospital every time I have a new case. One of them even made me a rewards card as a joke. I get it stamped every time I break a bone or need stitches. One more stamp this year, and I'll get a free foot-long hot dog at Ricardo's food truck on the pier.

In the past decade, I've been a server at Johnny B's Restaurant, a barista at a well-known coffee shop that still refuses to let me back inside, and a flag girl at a local speedway. I'm not very good at holding a real job. I'm even worse at dealing with customers. Even some of my clients.

That's why I prefer to be my own boss. Not that there's necessarily less drama, but I'm less likely to get fired for spitting in people's drinks or dumping pepper in food. Arrested and breaking bones, maybe, but let's take it one story at a time, shall we?

Like everything else I've ever done, I stumbled into being a PI when some hoity-toity friends of my parents were robbed. My parents took the robbery personally, deciding to add a security system to our then four-bedroom farmhouse. They kept on building from there.

My entire life I've relied on quick wit, charm, and sheer dumb luck to get by. My father always said that if it wasn't for dumb luck, I'd have no luck at all. Which is why I've never played the lottery or bought raffle tickets.

In my usual, headstrong way, I decided to prove my father wrong.

So, how did I get into this racket? Let me tell you...

* * *

Two days after my twelfth birthday, flashing red and blue lights and a forensics van lured me over to the Simmons house up the street. I guessed they were investigating the burglary I heard my parents discussing earlier. Before they caught me under the table and sent me outside to play.

Shy child I was, I approached one of the officers and said, "Excuse me."

He looked down his long, thin nose at me seeing nothing more than a scrawny kid in cut-offs, a striped t-shirt, and a baseball cap before he asked, "Do you live here?"

I shook my head. "No, sir, but I think—"

"Do you know who broke into the house?" he asked.

"No, sir, but I—"

He went inside and slammed the door in my face. It wasn't the first time someone slammed had a door in my face, and it wouldn't be the last.

Being a kid, I growled and stormed down the wide front steps. Then I realized no one else seemed to notice my presence. Using that to my advantage, I hid behind a giant hydrangea bush and inched my way around the house to search for an entry point. Surely, the burglars hadn't entered through the front door unless they had a key or jimmied the lock. The Simmons' had purchased a top-of-the-line alarm system back in January of that year. The whole neighborhood had endured false alarms for the first two weeks.

I managed to make it all the way around the four-thousand square foot house without anyone threatening to arrest me or sending me home. No signs of anything broken—windows, doors, or trellises—and the house was locked up tight. No indents in the soft earth from a ladder leaning against the building.

When the same long-nosed cop came out of the house, I walked straight up to him and announced, "This was an inside job."

Vagetti, as his name tag read, turned pink, which slowly darkened to purple. "Are you suggesting the Simmons robbed themselves?"

"Them or someone else who has a key," I said. "Maybe a friend or relative."

He stared at me for two long minutes, then asked, "Who are you?"

Not smart enough to keep my mouth shut and go home, I announced, "Dash Allman. I live nearby."

Vagetti smirked. "Dash?"

"Long story."

"You're Gus Allman's kid, aren't you? The one who got banned from the spray park for beating up a kid by the ice cream truck."

My face burned. "He was being rude. He barged into the front of the line, shoved a four-year-old out of the way, and demanded to be served first because he had to go home for dinner."

"You beat him up for that?" he asked.

"Actually, I beat him up after he stepped on the four-year old's hand and broke his finger. He also stole money from another kid to pay for his ice cream."

Vagetti's lips twisted like he wanted to laugh, just not in front of me. He shouted into the house, "Hey, Rookie, I've got a job for you."

Knowing I was about to be escorted from the property by another officer, I shook my head. "Don't you even want to hear my theory?"

He met my gaze and considered it for a whole second. "Nope."

"What's going on?" a younger man, about my dad's age, emerged from the house. This one's nametag read Carson. He was lean and hyped up, ready to do anything his superior officer requested. Grab coffee, lick his shoes...

"Take this kid home," Vagetti ordered.

Carson nodded. "Where do you live, kid?"

"This is Gus Allman's kid. The troublemaker. I'm sure you've dealt with her before."

"Dash?" Carson asked, lifting the brim of my hat a couple inches. "What are you doing here?"

"Same as you. Investigating a crime."

He chuckled. "Except that I have a gun and a badge."

"I'll have those one day."

"It's hard work being a cop, you know," Carson said.

Vagetti snorted. "It's harder keeping that nosy kid out of trouble. Don't let her out of your sight until she's inside her house and you see her parents."

"Yes, sir." Carson and I chorused in very different tones.

Once Vagetti returned inside the Simmons' house, Carson reached out a hand. "You probably don't remember me. I'm Officer Alex."

"Your badge says Carson."

"Alex Carson, at your service."

"Oh." I narrowed my eyes. "And how do you know me?"

"I'm the guy who drove you home from the beach after you ran away last time. We played Jimmy Buffett music over the police radio."

I grinned and broke into singing *Pencil Thin Moustache*, before I announced, "I know all his songs now. My favorites are *Margaritaville* and *Southern Cross*."

"Nice. Did you do know *Southern Cross* was a Crosby, Stills, and Nash song first?"

"Who are they?"

"We have work to do." He walked me toward a cruiser. "My favorite Buffett song is *Come Monday*. It reminds me of my wife. You married?"

I scrunched up my face. "Eww, no. I'm twelve."

Officer Alex laughed. "Hey, in some cultures, that's an acceptable age."

"That's gross. I'd rather be a kid. I'm sure those other girls would, too. Besides, if marriage is anything like the ones I've seen, you can keep it." I stopped next to the cruiser and met his gaze. "Can we not show up at my house in a police car again? Every time I do, I get grounded."

He placed his hand on top of my hat. "Sure, kid. It's a nice day. Let's go for a walk."

I arched one eyebrow. "You don't walk on bad days?"

"Most of the time I'm dealing with criminals and need to drive them to the station," he said. "That and I don't want my gun to rust or my radio to get wet."

"That's fair."

After we'd closed the gap to my house which was across from the field next to the Simmons' house, I asked, "Why won't Vagetti listen to my theory about the robbery?"

Officer Alex stopped. "What theory's that?"

"That it was an inside job."

He smiled in amusement. "Oh yeah? How do you figure that?"

"I walked around the house. All the doors and windows on the lower level are locked and there were no indentations in the ground to show someone used a ladder. Besides, the Simmons' have a top-of-the-line security system. Ever since they got it, the whole neighborhood hears it go off."

Officer Alex thought a moment. "What if the reason there are no indentations from a ladder is that the ground is dry?"

I shook my head. "Impossible. They water their lawn and flower beds every night from ten until midnight, unless they're hosting a party. The ground stays wet for hours."

"And how would you know that?"

"Me and Jenna are best friends. I've stayed over there lots of times since I was a kid. We got caught in the sprinklers a few times when we snuck out to the pool to swim under the stars."

"Didn't you set off the alarm?" he asked.

"It's new. They just got it after the first break-in."

Officer Alex pulled out a notebook. "The first break-in. When was that?"

"After Christmas. Whoever broke in, did it while they were at Mom and Dad's New Year's Eve party."

"Are you sure?"

"About the party or the alarm?"

He chuckled. "The alarm."

"Positive. They bought it a couple days after the party. So did everyone else on the street. The guy who sold them theirs came to our door. He was creepy. Kind of skinny and his fingernails were dirty. Not like a salesman at all. You might want to look into him."

Officer Alex grinned, writing more before he asked, "If I tell you that I'll check it out, will you promise to stay away from the Simmons' house until we finish our investigation?"

I looked away and crossed my fingers behind my back. "Maybe."

"Dash." His tone was as stern as his look.

I glanced back at the Simmons' three-story, white brick home and sighed. "Do you promise to fill me in if you find out anything that'll help the case?"

"How old are you?"

"Twelve."

"Then no."

I stomped my foot on the asphalt. "Oh, come on. I helped you. I'll bet if I was a private detective you'd help me."

"No, I wouldn't."

"Why not?"

Officer Alex placed a hand on my shoulder and steered me toward home. "Because PIs are pains in the butt who always want something for nothing."

"Whaddya mean?" I frowned, thinking of the detectives in the books I'd snuck off my mom's shelves.

"It starts out simple. A request for some background information. A name dropped here and there. That sort of thing. Next thing you know, I'm rescuing their sorry butts from a bike gang or a kindergarten class."

I stared. "A kindergarten class?"

"Trust me. I'd rather deal with the bike gang."

"Do you know any PIs I can talk to?" I asked, then quickly added. "For a school assignment."

"None who wouldn't tell you to come back when you were legal."

"What does that mean?"

His brown eyes widened. "When you can vote."

"Oh."

"Dashiell, what on earth have you done now?" my father barked.

Officer Alex gave my shoulder a warning squeeze. "Hey, Gus. She came over to the Simmons' house to see what was going on. I brought her home where she'd be safer and out of the way."

"Dashiell Agatha Allman." My mother's voice carried for blocks around us. "Get inside the house this instant."

"Funny how they don't notice I'm gone until the police drag me back," I muttered. "Thanks, Officer Alex."

He kept a grip on my shoulder. "Dash, here's my business card. Call me if you need anything, okay?"

"Like to talk to a real PI?"

"Except that."

I looked up into his kind eyes and nodded. "Thanks for walking me home. And for believing me."

"Anytime, kid."

After the obligatory parental rant and going to my room without dinner. My mom felt guilty enough at eight o'clock to bring me a sandwich, I lay on my bed and sketched the Simmons' yard from memory.

I was positive I'd looked everywhere a thief could possibly break into the house. Jenna and I had snuck into their house through every means possible—even by climbing over the morning glories covering the trellises. Between the two of us, we knew every inch of the floor plan. There was nowhere a grown up could get inside that we hadn't already tried.

What was I missing?

* * *

Wide awake, I lay in bed to wait until I heard laughter from my dad's favorite television show. The one he fell asleep to every night. Pressing my ear to the door, I heard my mom in their bedroom venting about my dad and I to her sister in Alaska. I hoped she wouldn't send me there for an "extended vacation." I hated snow. And polar bears.

Easing my window open, I crept out and inched over the ledge. Luckily, my room was on the ground floor. The only thing of concern beneath my window was the new rosebush my mom had planted. Presumably after she saw footprints in the garden near my window.

I managed to get past the thorns with a small scratch and clung to the shadows to make my way down the road to the Simmons' house. As usual, I didn't have a plan. No clue as to what I was looking for, or what I'd do if I found anything when I got there.

The bottle of water in my pocket gurgled as it shifted next to the chocolate bar. I'd come prepared to watch the house for an hour or so if I had to.

My feet hit the gravel shoulder of the road with a crunch. I stopped. Heart pounding and breath captive in my lungs. When I heard no other sounds in the night except the bull frogs in the pond across the road, I continued across the street to the freshly mown grass. That was when I stepped in something soft, slippery, and smelly.

Dead frog? Dog poop? Whatever it was, I needed to scrape it off my shoes before I got home, or I'd be busted. Shuffling my feet through the grass, I continued toward the wrought iron fence that surrounded the Simmons' yard, then paused.

Over or around?

If I went over, I could remain in the shadows. By going around, I risked setting off the lights above the garage. The Simmons were the first family on the street to have automatic lights. After being robbed twice in six months, I was sure they'd add other security features I didn't know about.

I chose to scale the wrought iron fence. At the top, I caught one of my pantlegs on a spike. Mom would really wonder about me if she found a rip near the crotch of my pants. I eased the fabric off the pointy metal and got over the top with no further problem.

Darting across the lawn, I made it to the swing set in back seconds before the kitchen light came on and cast a glow over the cement patio.

I sat on the hard plastic seat to catch my breath as Ian Simmons opened the fridge and patted his padded belly. The thick sandwich he crafted with layers of real ham, lettuce, pickles, and assorted condiments I didn't recognize, made my stomach growl for food. My mouth watered. The thin ham and cheese sandwich my mom brought me for dinner didn't even compare.

While I munched on my chocolate bar, I began to swing slowly. Not enough to be noticed, just to cool my skin in the summer heat.

Ian filled a large glass with milk, took his food off the kitchen island, and turned away. Raising one elbow, he turned off the light, then disappeared into the depths of the mansion.

Jenna's light was on. It flicked off, presumably because her mom reminded her it was a school night, and she needed to get some sleep. Within a minute, a dimmer light glowed in her second-floor window from the flashlight she kept hidden between her mattresses. Since a maid looked after the bedding, it was unlikely her mother knew about it.

I'd just taken a sip of water when the hissing began. Surprised, I lifted my feet above the ground. I'd never seen snakes in their backyard before. Hensel, the gardener, had some top-secret trick for keeping them away.

Or so Jenna bragged.

Before I realized what was happening, the sprinklers came on all around me. The ones that I'd told Officer Alex came on from ten o'clock until midnight every night. If I didn't get home soon, I'd be in far more danger than I'd be if I got caught by snakes or the police in Jenna's backyard.

I tossed the water bottle to one side and ran across the yard toward the fence. With the water from the sprinkler racing down the metal, there was no way I could climb it without getting hurt. I veered to the left and aimed for the interlocking stone driveway. The lights would come on and I was positive a police car was waiting somewhere along the street for trespassers to run by.

I didn't care.

Soaked and scared, I ducked my head and ran for home.

Sure enough, a set of lights came on behind me. A vehicle crept along the street a few feet from my heels. Gasping for breath, I raced toward my bedroom window, glad I'd left it open. All I had to do was hop through the opening and…

The window was closed. My bedroom light was on. My mother stood staring back at me with a look I could only describe as demonic. Busted.

"You promised not to go over there, Dash," a familiar voice spoke behind me. "What were you doing?"

"Surveillance." I turned around holding my hands up.

Officer Alex chuckled. "Put your hands down. You're not under arrest."

"I might as well be. I may never see you again. My parents are gonna put bars on my window after this. Just arrest me. Please. For my own safety."

He waved me toward his car and draped a towel over my shoulders. "I'll put in a special request that they go easy on you."

"They won't. I don't exactly have a clean record."

"I'm aware of that," he said, giving me a one-armed hug. "However, I believe in rehabilitation for petty criminals."

"They don't. How do I get rehabilitation instead of having them lock me up and throw away the key until I'm thirty?"

"You let me worry about that."

"It's too late," I wailed. "Did you see my mom's face? I'm a dead duck. She's gonna send me to Alaska to live with my aunt and a zillion polar bears."

Before Officer Alex could raise his hand to knock on the door, my dad opened it wearing a deep scowl. Mom stood behind him, her eyes narrow, red, and ready to shoot laser beams.

My parents, too mad to deal with me, sent me to my room. I didn't hesitate to make my escape from the stifling hostility in the kitchen, to the comfort of my bed. When I tried to open my window for fresh air. It wouldn't budge. Not only was it nailed shut, but my dad had put glue or something around the inside. I guessed it was around the outside as well to keep me from breaking out.

They weren't fooling around this time.

Shivering, I changed into pajamas, then lay across my bed and reached under my pillow for my diary. That was gone as well. Tears filled my eyes. I was about to throw a temper tantrum when I remembered I'd moved my diary to a new spot after catching my mom snooping in my room.

Honestly. What did she think I was up to? I was twelve.

I retrieved my diary from behind my dresser and fell across the bed to write about my day. Along with that, I made a list of suspects.

Ian Simmons, the dad, was an insurance broker or a banker, depending on who you asked. He was also Jenna's dad and liked me. Mostly from a distance.

Sophia Simmons, Jenna's mom, was what people politely called a philanthropist. I had to look that one up. She did give lots of money to people, but mostly salon workers, pool boys, gardeners, the country club staff, that sort of thing. She didn't like me at all, especially after Jenna and I stowed away in the back seat of her car one time to see where she went every Tuesday at two o'clock. When she discovered us, she dropped us off at the mall and told us to find our way home. Because we were ten, we turned it into an adventure. Rather than call for a ride, we took the bus and ended up two towns over.

Jenna and I weren't the only ones in trouble that day.

We'd been best friends since we met in kindergarten and discovered we lived practically across the street from each other. While her parents were convinced I was the troublemaker, some of the things we did were her idea. Taking the bus, for one. Hiding in the back seat of her mom's car was by far the worst.

Oh, we also met the guy Sophia was seeing and discovered it was our science teacher. Sure, we both got A's that year, but neither of us could look him in the eye without laughing. He shouldn't have called Sophia "Ducky Face" in front of us.

Hensel, the gardener, he had dark, creepy eyes and looked to be in his seventies. Not that I was a great judge of age. At twelve, everyone looked old. I also didn't like the way he looked at us when Jenna and I played in the yard, particularly in the pool.

The Simmons family had two maids: Manola and Erin. They treated Jenna and I like princesses and covered for us when we snuck out sometimes. It helped that we'd always bring them sweets, which they loved but could never buy often.

Then there was the cook, Esme was a thinner version of someone's grandmother who cooked for them and coddled them all the time. Not mine, but someone's.

The point was all those people had access to the stolen jewelry. They all lived in the house except the two maids, who rode the same bus Jenna and I took from the mall.

Before I could add more notes, someone pounded on the door with a heavy hand. My dad growled, "Go to bed."

Rather than causing more grief, I turned off my light and burrowed beneath the blankets hugging my diary.

"You're the only one I can trust," I whispered to the faux leather book. "I hope no one ever finds you, or I'm a double dead duck with orange sauce."

* * *

When neither of my parents said a word about my night time escapades the next morning, I should've known I was in serious trouble. Usually, one or both would rant and lose their minds.

That my mom had packed my lunch only confirmed my suspicions. Then she dropped the bombshell. "Officer Carson will be picking you up after school today."

I bowed my head. Straight to juvvie. No arrest. No trial. Did that mean I'd get out of schoolwork?

When I got on the bus, Jenna broke the news to me that we were no longer friends, and she wasn't allowed to sit next to me on the bus or in any classes. By lunch, word had spread that I'd stolen her parents' jewelry, and no one wanted to sit near me, let alone talk to me or work with me on projects.

After school, Officer Alex pulled up in his squad car. Head hanging, I held out my hands for him to cuff me before he tossed me in the backseat.

"What are you doing, Dash?" he asked.

"It's all over school that I stole the Simmons' jewelry. Jenna can't be my friend anymore, and no one else will talk to me. Just put me in solitary and throw away the key. I won't be getting any visitors."

Officer Alex opened the passenger door. "I could, if you want, but I think you'll like what I have planned better."

I narrowed my eyes. "I don't have to sit in the back?"

"It's not as much fun," he said. "I don't recommend it."

In the front seat, I got to savor the blast of the air-conditioned breeze that blew into my face. Once Officer Alex closed my door, I fastened my seat belt and realized at least fifty pairs of eyes were on me. Including Jenna Simmons'. While they watched, he got into the driver's seat and let me turn on the siren and lights. Every kid who grinned when I'd climbed into the police car, gawked in jealousy as we pulled away from the school.

Two block later, Officer Alex turned off the lights and siren before he said, "I'll bet they're not such jerks tomorrow."

My heart lighter, I laughed. "I'll bet you're right. Where are we going?"

"To the beach. There's a great place I'd like to show you."

That place turned out to be Ricardo's food truck. Ricardo Senior manned the grill. His son, Ricardo Junior, who looked about eighteen, took care of customers. They both had wide, white smiles, and chatted away in some language I didn't understand. For some reason, I felt completely at home next to their truck surrounded by wooden picnic tables and pink flamingoes.

"What'll you have?" Junior asked.

I was overwhelmed by the menu choices, until the officer chuckled and asked for two breakfast dogs and sodas. We sat at the end of the pier eating gigantic hot dogs covered with shredded cheese, hashbrowns, tomato, bacon, and a fried egg. Both of us swung our legs over the water as if to tempt the fish below.

"You're not one of those creepy guys who's gonna sell me to someone in another country, are you?" I asked, as egg yolk ran down my chin.

"Absolutely not. I swear on my badge and my two little girls."

"You have little girls?"

"Jayde and Belinda," he said. "They're two and six months old. I'm hoping to have more kids, but probably not for a few years. Do you have any brothers or sisters?"

I shook my head. "Nope. If I do, they ran away a long time ago."

Officer Alex sipped his soda. "You and your parents don't get along very well, do you?"

I dropped a piece of bun into the water for the fish. "That's an understatement."

"You have quite the vocabulary for a twelve-year-old."

"I read a lot," I told him. "Mysteries mostly. And I like to learn things, which makes my parents crazy. They say I'm too nosy, and should focus on my schoolwork and chores instead."

He pointed to a couple fish nibbling at my bread chunk, then tossed in a second one before asking, "Do you like school?"

"I like learning stuff, but the kids are annoying. They're so fake. I hate that we have to work with partners. Jenna was the only one I liked working with and now we're not friends anymore."

"Did your parents tell you that?"

I shook my head as the fish reappeared for more bread. "She did on the bus this morning. Now everyone knows, and they all hate me."

"After you got to turn on the lights and siren in my car? I doubt that. Jenna Simmons isn't cool compared to that."

"Her family has a pool."

"Okay, so she's got a pool. You're a lot more interesting."

I snorted. "I'm twelve. No one thinks twelve-year-olds are interesting. Not even other twelve-year-olds."

Officer Alex burst out laughing. "I suppose."

"Are you sure my parents didn't tell you to lock me up?" I asked.

He met my gaze. "Actually, they wanted me to talk to you because they don't know what to do with you."

"And you do?"

He crumbled the last of his bun and sprinkled the crumbs over the water. "Not exactly."

"Then what are we doing here?"

He met my gaze. "Who do you suspect in the Simmons' case?"

"Really?" My eyes grew wide.

"You seem like a smart, observant kid, and you know the family way better than I do. Tell me what you think."

I filled him in on everything I'd written in my diary. The whole time I talked, he took notes and asked questions. He listened to every word I said and didn't just write me off as a dumb kid. Even when I mentioned Jenna had a way older brother, but I'd never met him, and no one ever talked about him.

"I think he's the family sheep dog," I told him.

"Black sheep," he corrected. "I'll check that out, thanks."

By the time Officer Alex drove me home, I felt like I was a part of something I'd only ever dreamed of.

As we drove past the Simmons' house, I looked to see if Jenna was on her swing in the backyard sulking. There were about ten kids all gathered at her pool. My heart began to sink again—until I spotted a figure in the woods behind their house.

"Stop!" I shouted.

By the time Officer Alex pulled over, we were past the house but in full sight of the bullfrog pond. A man broke through the trees and into the open field.

"That's who I saw behind their house!"

"Stay here," Officer Alex ordered. Jumping out of the car, he ran into the ditch, shouting for the man to stop.

I reached for the door handle, then paused when the radio crackled. He was calling into headquarters, but his radio kept cutting out. I picked up the mic and took a deep breath. "This is Dash Allman. Officer Alex is requesting backup at 1600 Sunset Court. He's in hot pursuit of a suspect running through the trees away from the Simmons' house."

I looked up in time to see the other man pull something out of his pocket. "It looks like he has a gun! Hurry!"

There was a crack, and the other man disappeared into the tall grass like he'd fallen. Seconds later, Officer Alex also vanished. I screamed into the mic before abandoning the safety of the police car and running into the ditch. I expected to see both men lying in the grass covered in blood.

Instead, they were gone.

"What's going on?" I shouted. "Where are you?"

"Dash, can you hear me?" Officer Alex called out.

I looked around, still unable to see him. "Yes. Where are you?"

"Stay back. We're in a sinkhole. If you come closer, you'll fall in."

"A sinkhole?" I wanted to add "cool" but it wasn't the time or place. I got onto my belly and crawled toward the gaping hole in the field. Peering over the edge, I saw Officer Alex holding another man's head out of water. Both men were wet and muddy as more water trickled down the walls around them.

"Go back to the car and radio for help," he instructed. "Tell them to send a firetruck so we can get out of here. This guy's hurt but I can't tell how bad."

"Are you at least standing on the bottom?" I asked.

"Kneeling for now, but the water's coming in from the pond and the underground spring," he said. "You need to hurry, Dash."

Inching back from the edge, I got to my feet and ran back the way I came. I sobbed with each step. I'd never seen a real sinkhole before. This one was threatening to take away my one friend in the whole wide world.

I crawled into the police car as two more pulled up behind it. Ignoring them, I told the dispatcher about the sinkhole and to send a firetruck and an ambulance. Then the waterworks started as I begged her, "Hurry! Please! Officer Alex is down there and the hole's filling with water."

Officer Vagetti crouched near the door as I wiped my face with my bare arm and asked, "Where are they, kid?"

"I'll show you."

He shook head. "We've got this, Dash. I don't want anyone else to get hurt. How far into the field are they?"

I pointed to a large rock on the far side of the pond. "Past that rock and to the left. He's trying to keep the other guy from drowning, but..." I hiccupped and sobbed at the same time.

Vagetti nodded. "It's okay, kiddo. Carson's one of ours. We'll save him."

For the first time since I met the guy, I wanted to hug him. I settled for whispering a watery, "Thank you."

He left another officer to keep an eye on me and marched across the field with his men. They were halfway to the sinkhole when two firetrucks arrived. The firefighters followed them, carrying two long ladders into the field.

I watched from the car as they slid the ladders into the hole. Holding my breath, I was terrified the sink hole would swallow everyone and Officer Alex's little girls would grow up without a dad.

"What's going on?" a woman asked.

I didn't answer. Nor did I take my gaze off the emergency responders.

The officer Vagetti asked to keep an eye on me, told me to get out of the car. I nodded and barely looked at my parents, who didn't seem to know if they should be happy to see me or mad I was mixed up in police business.

It was my father who grabbed me by the shoulders and shook me as he asked, "What did you do this time?"

"Officer Alex was chasing a guy in the field, and they fell into a sinkhole," I told them, my voice quivering.

The officer chuckled. "She's being modest. Your daughter's quick thinking saved them both. She called for backup, a firetruck, and an ambulance. They're coming out now."

"You can see them? Are they okay?" I asked.

He nodded as I ran toward him and lifted me up in time to see Officer Alex emerge from the hole. He was wet and muddy, but he didn't seem hurt.

Without thinking, I hugged the officer and sputtered my thanks as I cried on his shoulder. One of those ugly cries that kids do when they're so happy they have no words.

"Go home with your mom and dad," he told me after several awkward minutes and a huge hug. "I'm sure Officer Alex will call you once he gets checked out at the hospital."

"He's okay, isn't he?" My sobs were punctuated by a couple more hiccups.

He nodded. "The doctor will make sure he has no injuries before they let him leave. I'll tell him to give you a call as soon as he can."

My parents walked me home with little to say. Praise as one of those things they had yet to master. Even after I changed clothes and sat with them in the livingroom for pie and ice cream, I thought they'd at least be thankful I was okay. Or proud that I'd helped save two men's lives.

Nothing.

My dad did take the nails out of my window while I had a bath. I was in bed before eight and fell into a dreamless sleep.

* * *

"Are you awake?" my mom asked softly.

I struggled to open one eye. The other one refused to co-operate. "Kinda."

"Your dad's making pancakes and bacon. I hope you're hungry."

"I died in the sinkhole, didn't I?" I asked.

My mom laughed. A sound I hadn't heard in a long time. "No, silly, you're very much alive. Get dressed and meet us in the..." She paused, then rummaged through my closet and pulled out the frilliest piece of cotton candy fluff that I'd ever seen. "Put this on."

"What is it?"

"A dress. And you're going to wear it to breakfast. Now, hurry up."

I pinched my arm. "Ouch." If I wasn't dreaming, then what was going on? I'd heard of a show called The Twilight Zone. Is that where I was now?

Tossing the fluffy pink fabric on the floor and stepping on it, I opted for my favorite cut offs and t-shirt with a pink flamingo on the front. Darn if I was dressing up for pancakes and bacon only to have her get mad for getting syrup on my clothes.

My mom's face fell when I walked into the kitchen. She was surrounded by television cameras, microphones, and photographers.

"What's going on?" I asked, taking a step back as my eyes grew wide.

A tall man with teeth so perfect they looked fake, shoved a microphone in front of my face and asked, "How does it feel to be a hero, Dashiell? You save the lives of both Officer Alex Carson and Cray Simmons."

"Cray Simmons?" I frowned as I backed away. "Who's that?"

The grown-ups burst into laughter. Cheeks burning, I wove between them like a high school quarterback and ran out into the yard barefoot. The driveway and street in front of our house were full of vehicles. News vans, fancy cars with vanity plates, rusty beaters, police cars...

When Officer Alex waved from the police car, I wiped my arm across my face, then ran toward him. I jumped into the passenger seat, and said, "Get me out of here."

He made a face. "I'd love to, but your parents invited me for breakfast. I see we won't be eating alone."

"Nope. There are sharks in the kitchen. Reporters everywhere! Can you believe she wanted me to wear some frilly pink dress? It was hideous. I would've looked like some weird bird."

"Says the girl wearing a pink flamingo shirt."

I reached to open the door to escape before I remembered something and asked, "Hey, who's Cray Simmons?"

"Remember you mentioned Jenna had a brother you'd never met? He's the bad guy you helped us nab. Ian's son from his first marriage who wanted his share of the family fortune up front," he said.

"Well, that's not fair."

"What do you mean?"

"How am I supposed to solve a case when I had no idea the guy was in town, or that he was even a suspect?"

"That's the way police work goes, Dash."

"Did you know about him?"

"I did."

"Then why didn't you tell me?"

He shook his head. "Because you're twelve and not a police officer."

"Not yet," I growled.

Officer Alex chuckled, then ruffled my hair. "What do you say we put our brave faces on and join the chaos at your house? I don't know about you, but I love pancakes."

"There's bacon, too."

"My two favorite food groups," he said.

"Mine, too."

"Good. Then let's go eat and pretend there are no sharks and we're not really heroes. We're just hungry detectives."

"Deal," I told him.

As we walked toward my house, I had one last question. "Can I work with you on your next case?"

He shook his head. "Not until you're a trained police officer."

"Or a private detective like Dick Tracy?"

"Don't push it." He held the door open as a barrage of questions greeted us. Most of them from my parents.

Just the Beginning...

ON BEACH TIME

DIANE BATOR

ASH ALLMAN MYSTERIES BOOK 2

On Beach Time

Dash Allman PI, Book 2

Diane Bator

Escape With a Writer Publishing

My phone fell off the table while Jimmy Buffett serenaded me about looking for salt over my earbuds. I reached to pick it up but was stopped by a shiny, black loafer resting on the back of my only good hand, the right one. There was only one man I knew who wore Brunello Cucinelli loafers with tassels.

"Phil. Buddy. What's up?" I asked, still doing an awkward version of Triangle Pose while waving my purple cast in the air. Good thing I'd opted to get dressed that morning.

"Your time, Dash. Say your prayers. I can't believe your parents named you that. Didn't they like you?"

The joke in my family was that my mom hated me, but loved Dashiell Hammett, which really sucked for the little girl she named Dashiell Agatha Allman. Not funny. The nickname Dash did make me feel faster though.

I smirked and stood as he released my hand. "Seriously? That joke's as old as you are."

He gripped my throat with his left hand before I could back away. A freshly broken left wrist from a fall while chasing a bad guy last night had made me slower than normal. Too bad I hadn't listened when the doctor instructed me to fill the prescription of painkillers. I made a mental note to add that to my list—if Phil didn't kill me.

"Let's make a deal," he said, pulling my face to within two inches of his. "You solve a case for me, and I won't kill you."

I weighed my pros and cons. Pay rent. Solve a case. Live a little longer. Go work at the Seaglass Pub serving drinks while wearing a short skirt for tips.

"What's the case?" I croaked, struggling to breathe.

Phil Turner eased his grip so I could inhale, but he didn't let me go. "Follow my wife and see what she's up to."

Trying to swallow, I asked, "Affair?"

His grip tightened as his spittle hit me right below the eye. "Not in a million years. You got that, Dash?"

"Yup," came out barely a squeak.

This time, he released me, shoving me against the kitchen table. I really hated it when the creeps knew where I lived. I picked up my phone before he or the goon who blocked my doorway could step on it.

Phil, mid-sixties and dressed like a lawyer even though he "sold used cars", straightened his tie. "Yolanda's been meeting some other chick. Usually, she tells me her business, but this time she clams up when I ask what's going on. Something's up."

"Maybe she's planning you a surprise birthday party."

"My birthday's in December. This here's July."

I was willing to wager a black eye or two had made Yolanda wary and she had a Plan B. "Okay. Where do they meet?"

Phil glanced back at the sandy-haired goon in the gray bespoke suit who stepped forward and flicked a business card from his jacket pocket in one motion.

"Cool trick," I mused. "You do magic?"

The Goon stepped back his expression somber except for a slight eyebrow raise.

"Tough room." I glanced at the card.

"Her name's Candy and there's a number, but that's it," Phil told me.

Pale pink with white stripes, or white with pale pink stripes, and an almost velvety texture. Expensive. My first guesses ranged from makeup to something naughty. I hiked up a bra strap as it slid over my shoulder from beneath my tank top, then glanced up at him and asked the obvious, "Did you call the number?"

"You're the people person. That's your job."

"Of course, it is." Blowing a curly strand of bleached blonde hair off my face, I punched the numbers into my phone.

The voice that answered was sultry, husky, and made me even more curious. "Candy. How can I help you?"

My mouth flapped a couple times before my brief two class background in improv kicked in. "Hi, Candy. I'm Ashley. A friend gave me your card and told me to call you."

"Oh yeah? How come?" she asked, sounding much cooler than I was at the moment.

I winced when Phil waved a hand expectantly. "I told her I needed someone to talk to and she handed me this pink striped card. Nice shade of pink. Is it cotton candy?"

"Peppermint. I'll be right over. Where are you?" she asked.

"Not here. Mayberry Café at two p.m.?" A quick glance at the clock confirmed it was nearly noon. That gave me time to do some research and struggle into clean clothes.

"I know it. See you there."

Before I'd removed the phone from my ear, Phil was less than six inches away. "Well?"

I leaned away from the garlic and onions he breathed on me as my phone rang again. I let it go to voice mail as I snapped, "You heard me. Mayberry Café at two o'clock."

"Who is she?" he asked. "What does she do?"

"How should I know?" I wound around the table to my makeshift office on the couch and reached for my laptop. A one-handed reverse phone search came up empty. Unlisted. Candy could've been anything or anyone. Just like Phil.

"I'm coming with you to meet her." He hovered between the couch and the table.

"How about you give me a lift and wait in the car? I'll pick a seat near the window. That way you can keep an eye on both of us but not scare her off, so I can find out for both of us."

He grumbled. "I'll be back at quarter to two. You'd better be here, or our deal is off."

I touched my throat, then locked the front door behind him. Only after he left did I put the music back on. Before I could relax enough to bust out a couple dance moves, my phone rang. No caller ID. My stomach squirmed as I answered.

"Forget Mayberry," Candy said. "Meet me at the Sandcastle Diner on the pier in ten minutes."

My eyes grew wide. "Wait. How do you know I—?"

"Don't be late, Dash."

The call ended and suddenly Jimmy was crooning about margaritas. I could've used one about then. Instead, I took some over the counter pain meds before the day got any stranger. As I rubbed the cast on my left arm absently, I had an odd realization.

Who would've thought a broken wrist could lead to a complete interrogation of my life choices? The doctor at the hospital asked a long list of very personal questions.

Was my spouse violent at times and did he drink? I don't have one.

Did my boyfriend get angry often? I avoid dating. Long story.

Did either of my parents have dementia accompanied by angry outbursts? Nope. They were living it up in Costa Rica on holidays. They weren't even in town.

I'd broken bones before, so I knew this wasn't a standard line of questioning. Most of the hospital staff knew me by name, or at least reputation. They'd taken to giving me gold stars every time I didn't break a bone. Three more gold stars and I'd get a free hot dog at Ricardo's food truck on the pier.

No way would I share that hot dog with Phil. Not after today.

I wasn't about to tell him Candy had returned my call, either. Grabbing my small purse with the long strap, I draped it across my shoulders and headed for the pier.

* * *

Candy was a breeze to spot. There weren't many women dressed like Corporation Barbie in the diner on the pier. Everyone else wore flip flops, shorts, and T-shirts promoting every location in the country imaginable. Only one wore four-inch pink Manolo Blahnik shoes with glittering buckles on the toes and a matching pink Gucci suit capped off by a wide-brimmed black hat with matching peppermint pink ribbon. The only thing out of place were the unmanicured fingernails she tried to hide behind the soda she sipped.

Did I mention my mystery-loving Mama also ran a high fashion magazine? Having a beer-drinking, tattooed daughter who worked with slimeballs and deadbeats didn't exactly keep me in her good graces on a regular basis. Especially when I ended up in the emergency room every week or two.

"How did you know who I was?" I asked, slipping onto the bench across the table from her.

Her pink lips curved into a sly smile. "Easy. I called you back and got your voicemail."

So much for having the upper hand.

"Phil Turner sent you, didn't he?" Candy asked.

"Why do you say that?" I forced a fake air of innocence.

Her fingertips brushed my neck. "The signature bruises."

I inched away. "Are you planning to help his wife get away from him?"

"My plans don't concern you." She smiled. "His wife's plans may. I would suggest that if he owes you money to get it up front."

With that, she tossed a couple bills on the table. More than enough to pay for her soda. I gnawed on the inside of my cheek as she sashayed across the diner and out the door. Something about her bothered me. Partly the fact her entire wardrobe cost more than my rent. Partly because I had a gut feeling she was as phony as Phil was greedy.

I sat back and waved off the server when she asked if I wanted to order anything. She took the cash then returned with the change just as my stomach rumbled. Sliding the change into my hand, I wandered back up the pier and across the sand to my favorite food truck to grab a hot dog.

Phil didn't owe me money, but Candy's inference that I should get paid upfront disturbed me.

Back at my beach house, I changed out of my tank top with the fresh mustard blob on it and settled for a relatively clean blue one. I continued to search for any clues about Candy before deciding to start at square one. Yolanda Turner.

Aside from being Phil's wife, she had a small presence on social media to promote her artwork. Not a great artist, as far as I was concerned, but people seemed to like her work. A couple images of her paintings, mostly of flowers and seashells, had sold banners beneath them. Nowhere in her social media did I see any sign of Candy. Someone like her would be hard to miss, wouldn't she?

A quick glance at the clock confirmed my more immediate fear. It was quarter to two. Phil and his goon would return any minute to take me to Mayberry Café. He'd be peeved when Candy was a no-show, but I figured I should just let that play out and keep him in public.

I touched my throat and thought of wearing a jaunty scarf. Until the vision of him using it to send me to my demise entered my mind. Best to go *au natural*.

* * *

By 2:05pm, I realized Phil wasn't going to show up and I was off the hook. Happy not to have to smell his rancid breath again, I began to grow more concerned with each minute that ticked past. Where was he?

Returning to my computer, I continued to research. I got lost down an electronic rabbit hold until my gaze wandered back to my phone around three o'clock. I had two options. I could call Phil to check up on him and face more abuse, or head down to the Mayberry Café solo to see if anyone had seen he or Candy. Before I could scrounge a coin out of the couch cushions to flip, the doorbell rang.

Not Phil. He was more the barge right in type.

I raked my fingers through my unruly hair in case of a potential customer and opened it. "Police?"

Two officers, one tanned and athletic, the other his complete opposite, stood on my front step. I knew the pale one. Officer Alex Carson and I went way back. Literally to when I was a kid.

The athletic officer I'd never met spoke first. "We're looking for Doshell Allman." He pronounced my first name as two separate words.

"It's Dashiell. Dash, for short," I told him.

Athletic laughed. From his deep tan, I guessed he was a surfer in his time off. "Didn't your mother like you?"

I grimaced. "That's my joke. Can I help you?"

Carson rolled his eyes. "We understand Phil Turner was here earlier today. Can you tell us what your meeting with him was about?"

"Nope." I wished I had put on a touch of makeup though. The tall cop was cute in a macho sort of way.

Athletic exchanged glances with Pasty. "Why not?"

"He was my client. That information is privileged."

"Even if he's dead?" Carson asked, pulling out a notebook.

My eyes grew wide, and my breath stuck in my throat. I gave a cough to kickstart my body. "He's what?"

Athletic pulled out his phone and swiped at the screen a couple times before he turned it toward me. "Is this Phil?"

I sucked in a sharp breath. "Except for that hole in his forehead, it looks just like him. Do you know who shot him?"

"That's privileged, Dash," Carson said. "You know that."

Since my wrist was throbbing, I held it close to my chest rubbing the cast absently. I was glad Carson couldn't see me giving him the finger since none of my fingers could move.

His partner grimaced. "We thought you might know. Was he afraid someone might do this?"

"If he was, he never told me."

"What did he tell you?" Athletic asked. "Now that he's dead, I doubt it matters if you tell us."

I spit out the first little white lie I could come up with, which I knew from the local rumor mill wasn't far off base. "He thought his partner was cheating him."

"His wife?"

Struggling, I stuck to something I knew was the truth. "Business. He was supposed to pick me up for a meeting at the Mayberry Café at two o'clock. He never showed. Since it's nearly three, I'd guess whoever we were meeting is long gone by now."

Officer Carson closed his notebook and stuck it in his pocket. "Phil didn't give you a name?"

"Nope." Another truth. I was on a roll.

Athletic took a business card from his pocket. "If you happen to find out anything, please give me a call."

I glanced at the card then gave him a quick once over before I smiled. "Sure thing, Officer Robert Gwynn."

"Call me Rob. See you later, Dash." Athletic turned and walked down the sidewalk toward the street.

That would imply familiarity I wasn't ready for. I did peer around Carson for a better look though. Yup. I'd hang onto his card. Just in case.

"You'd better not be playing us, Dash," Carson kept his voice low. "We know Phil Turner was murdered. Since you were one of the last people to see him, you're at the top of our list."

"Gee, don't I feel special." I stared after him when he left, but not the way I'd ogled Officer Athletic. Sure, I'd been a suspect before, but not for shooting anyone. As much as I'd wanted Phil dead, or at least out of my life, I was in the clear on this one.

Returning to my computer, I grabbed a stack of sticky notes. The cheap kind. Not the ones that stayed put when you pressed them to a wall. Problem was they also refused to stick to the table so I could write on them.

My suspect list was short: Yolanda, Phil's wife; Candy; and Phil's goon whose name I could never seem to remember. In the brief time from when Phil had left my beach house to when he died, they were the only three people who seemed logical. Well, the only three I knew of. Since Pasty hadn't mentioned a second body, it wasn't a stretch to think the Goon was involved somehow.

Candy's card stared at me from near my computer. Yeah, I could picture her with a cute little pearl-handled Derringer pistol. Although, with my luck, she was probably more the Glock type. I stuck her card in the back pocket of my cut-off shorts.

I decided to visit the widow first. If I couldn't talk to her, the Goon would likely be close by, and I could see what he knew. Leaving the house, I walked my moped down the front walk and realized I should've taken another painkiller.

Yes, I drive a moped. Not the best thing to ride in a high-speed chase scenario, but I didn't get involved in those often. Besides, it made me look approachable, and it was cheap on gas. The vibration and hitting the turn signal was going to hurt my wrist like crazy. If Yolanda offered me a drink, I'd probably accept. The stiffer, the better.

Phil and Yolanda lived ten miles away in a gated community. Lucky for me, mopeds fit on bike paths. I squeezed through a half-open gate and rode toward their house as if I belonged there. My only obstacle was that I needed to hide behind a large tree to wait for Officers Carson and Athletic to leave once they'd dropped off the Goon.

Interesting. Was he a witness to the crime?

Taking off my helmet, I fluffed up my flat curls and marched up to the bright red front door. I paused to apply a layer of pale pink lip gloss, which was no easy feat with one good hand and one throbbing one, then rang the doorbell.

Within seconds, the Goon filled the doorway. One look at me and he began to slam it shut. "Not now."

I stuck my foot next to the doorjamb while calling out, "I just want to offer my sympathies to the widow. I won't stay long. I promise."

This time, the door opened slowly. The Goon was replaced by a woman a couple inches shorter than me with bright red hair and more makeup than a circus clown. Not the grieving widow I'd pictured. No redness or raccoon eyes.

"Yolanda?" I raised my eyebrows. "You look different."

She frowned. "Dash. I should've known you'd show up. You and Phil were always thick as thieves."

"Only because I busted him a couple times and he kept hiring me anyway."

Yolanda stepped back with a sigh. "Come in before the neighbors see you and call the police. Who beat you up this time?"

"Some kid at the skateboard park," I told her as I raised my cast.

The Goon closed the door behind me as I followed Yolanda across the terra cotta tiles toward the sunroom—sorry, lanai—that faced the beach out back. I'd been reprimanded half a dozen times by Phil on what the room was called.

"Gerald, can you please fetch us a couple drinks? Scotch. Neat," she said.

Although Scotch was not my poison of choice, I held up a finger. "I'll have ice."

Gerald scowled, presumably at the added three seconds of work—or my mere presence—then left the room. Somewhere down the hall, an unseen clock ticked.

"I'm sorry to hear about Phil," I started with the obvious platitude.

She rolled her bright green eyes and groaned. "Oh, please. Don't patronize me. That man was as mean to you as he ever was to me."

"Is that why you were leaving him?"

Yolanda raised her ultra-thin eyebrows. "Did he tell you that?"

I shook my head. "All he said was that you were meeting some woman, and gave me her card."

For a redhead with translucent skin, she turned deathly pale. Since she didn't have the benefit of a drink or ice to add moisture to her mouth, I continued to tell her about meeting Candy and how Phil was supposed to pick me up at quarter to two. Once all my cards were on the table, she sat back and blew out a long breath.

Gerald returned and handed me a drink before giving the other glass to Yolanda.

She downed it in one gulp.

I raised my eyebrows in surprise.

Without a word, he touched her hand before taking her glass and leaving the room like it was a routine. I guessed he'd return in a couple minutes, which meant I didn't have time to waste.

"He was right," she whispered, placing the tips of her fingers against her throat. "I was planning to leave. Candy works for a group that helps women escape abusive situations."

"I had a hunch." Although Candy's expensive ensemble still puzzled me. I couldn't figure out what I was missing.

"Once I was in a safe house and out of danger, I planned to file the divorce papers and be done with that monster for good," she explained.

I smirked. "Unless he dragged it out for years or had you sign some ridiculous pre-nup."

Gerald returned just in time. Yolanda grabbed the glass and downed the second drink like it was lemonade on a sweltering summer day.

Once he'd left the room for a third time, she glared at me and asked, "How did you know?"

I raised my eyebrows. "About the pre-nup? I'm a PI. I hear all about them and see the loopholes people try to find to escape them. I imagine yours says you'd get nothing if you leave him or cheat on him."

Yolanda sank back into the chair like she wanted to disappear. Tears filled her eyes as her chin quivered. "You're better than I thought."

"You need to leave now," Gerald said, handing Yolanda his kerchief and a fresh drink.

I gawked. It was the first time I'd heard him speak since we met five years earlier. His voice was deeper than I'd expected. As the ticking clock struck four, I had an a-ha moment. "You two?"

He turned to Yolanda who dabbed at her eyes transferring half her mascara and green eyeshadow to the pale pink kerchief. When she reached for his hand, he took it and gave a squeeze.

"Yes," she whispered. "He had to look after me so many times after Phil..." She broke down sobbing.

Gerald took the glass from her hand and brushed the hair out of her face. "I fell in love with her. Phil didn't deserve her, but I didn't kill him. I wanted to, especially after the last time when he nearly killed her. She was in hospital for days."

"Hospital?" My back stiffened, yet I still couldn't connect the elusive dots. "Is that where you met Candy."

Yolanda gave a small laugh. "Yeah, I knew they had volunteers, but I didn't think they still called them Candy Stripers."

"They don't, but it's a neat gimmick. I need to make a call. Thanks for your help," I told them, then set my untouched drink on a side table and got up. Crossing the room, I paused in the entryway near the large grandfather clock. "Could I use the washroom?"

Gerald ushered me to the nearest powder room, then returned to the lanai.

I locked the door behind me, pulled out Candy's card, and sat on the toilet lid to read it again. That niggly thing that had bothered me all afternoon was right in front of my face on that card. A lone little period. Certainly not visible at first glance. I'd probably mentally brushed it off as a piece of lint from Gerald's pocket and ignored it.

Right behind the letter C. While everyone called her Candy, the card really read, "C. ANDY."

I cursed and covered my face with both hands. Last night when I was in the emergency room, a young doctor had tended to me. Doctor Carl Andy. My broken wrist brought on his barrage of questions about my entire life. While the interrogation seemed harmless enough at the time, I tried to picture Doctor Carl in drag. The only thing I had left to do was call Candy to confirm my suspicions.

And possibly Officer Carson or Athletic. I refused to call him Rob. Not yet.

I splashed my face with cold water and left Yolanda and Gerald to carry on.

* * *

We agreed to meet at six o'clock at the Sandcastle Diner. I'd even gone to the trouble of reserving a table for two near the window within sight of two "fishermen." I'd also ordered a drink. A margarita. I tried to lick the salt off my finger while I waited, but my hand shook too badly. I was scared I'd poke my eye with a salty finger. Grace was not my greatest asset.

Candy was right on time. As she sauntered across the room wearing the same suit and hat as earlier, she turned the heads of both men and women. She slid into the booth next to me, leaving her wide-brimmed hat on her head. Did she have a camera hidden in it for blackmail purposes? If so, I'd have to ask where she got it.

"Did you change your mind about needing my help?" she asked.

I forced myself to think of something sad. Picturing Yolanda in hospital broken and battered did it. I magically conjured up tears before I told her, "Phil died."

Candy gasped, but it was only for show. Her eyes betrayed her. She already knew. "Phil Turner? I'm sorry to hear that. Yolanda never told me."

Grabbing a napkin, I wiped my eyes. Certainly not as elegantly as the grieving widow had. I was a much uglier crier. Good thing I wore ten less coats of makeups than she did.

"I stopped by to check on her earlier," I told Candy. "She's not taking it well. I hope she doesn't do anything stupid."

That got her attention. "Oh, dear. You mean like harming herself?"

"She's pretty devastated."

Candy shook her head. "No. She can't be."

"Why not?" I asked, my tears drying up as magically as they'd started.

"That was what she wanted." C. Andy placed her pink handbag on the table and began to rummage through it.

Since she was visibly distressed and already distracted, I decided to play my trump card. "I know who you are."

I didn't have to say more. Doctor Carl Andy's hospital identification card fell onto the table next to my good hand. I picked it up and compared the image of the thin, light-skinned man I'd met in the emergency room to the perfectly put together woman seated across from me.

"It's not what you think," he said, not even falling out of character.

I held my hand up to stop the officer at the next table from jumping to his feet and taking over too soon. "Then maybe you'd better enlighten me."

Carl batted his fake eyelashes and wiped real tears away before he told me, "My stepfather abused my mom when I was a kid. I was too weak to do anything about it, but I wanted to kill that man so badly."

"You were just a kid."

"I was a spineless jellyfish, but I'm not anymore." Reaching into the handbag, he pulled out a small, silver-plated Cobra Derringer .22 with pearl grips barely visible before he wrapped his hand around them.

"Huh. My first guess was right." Too bad I couldn't brag about it to anyone.

"About what?" he asked.

"Doesn't matter now."

Hiding his left hand discretely behind his purse, he aimed the barrel at me. "In my medical residency, I saw so many battered women and kids that it made me physically ill. Finally, I decided to do something about it."

"I see. So, you dressed in drag, became Candy, and offered to help them escape bad situations."

"Exactly."

"Then you killed their abusers, so they'd be safe," I added.

He held up his index finger about to straighten me out. That's when I realized what was off about Candy. The lack of a flawless manicure. Carl couldn't get his nails done without being found out sooner. How long had he been able to pull off the masquerade?

"It's not what you think," Carl insisted. "I save innocent women and children. I'm an Angel of Mercy. Those men all get what's coming to them. It's just a matter of time. Now, if you don't mind, you and I are going to take a walk to the end of the pier, then I'll report a drowning."

I winced. "Except I spent seven years on swim team. I'm a strong swimmer."

Carl flashed a sweet smile. "Not with a bullet in your head."

"Okay, that sounded like a threat to me." Officer Athletic hauled Carl to his high heels.

Officer Carson slapped on the handcuffs with gusto. He seemed thrilled to be able to arrest a perp they'd been actively seeking for a couple years now. While Alex Carson and two other officers walked Carl, still wearing his stilettos, out to a cruiser, Officer Athletic took a seat across the table.

"You okay?" he asked.

I held out my right hand, palm facing the table and wobbled it. "My legs are shaking, and I probably can't stand up yet."

He grinned. "At least you don't have any more broken bones."

My face burned as I reached for my margarita. Had he investigated me as a suspect?

"My name's Rob." He held out a strong, tanned hand. Rippling muscles. No wedding ring. Perfect smile.

I hesitated, then shook. "You said that earlier. I'm Dash."

He had mahogany eyes that seemed to see straight inside me. "I'm off duty at ten. You want to grab a drink?"

"I already have one," I told him, holding up my margarita.

Rob smiled, his eyes crinkling in the corners as though I amused him. "I meant a real one."

As a pleasant shiver swept through my body, I had a feeling this man could be seriously fun trouble. Emphasis on the trouble. "Ten it is."

"I'll pick you up at your place." He winked, then stood and walked slowly toward the exit as though he knew me and every other woman in the diner were watching.

I'd need another margarita and couple cold showers when I got home. Except one thing still bothered me. I tossed some money on the table then took off after Officer Athletic. Rob.

"We're not done here," I panted as I caught up to him.

He smirked, then asked, "Did you miss the part where I said I'd pick you up when I got off work?"

"Not that. Candy...Carl... Whoever that is said that Yolanda wanted Phil dead."

Rob knitted his eyebrows together and frowned. "Do you think Yolanda paid Candy to kill Phil?"

"It was either her or Gerald. They both had good reasons."

Now he looked even more confused. "Gerald? Why would Phil's assistant want him dead?"

I clapped a hand over my eyes. "Because he's not an assistant, he was Phil's bodyguard. He and Yolanda were having an affair despite the fact she and Phil had a pre-nup stating if she cheated on him or left him, she'd get nothing. Have you seen their house? I'm sure the bank account matches. That's a lot for anyone to give up."

Rob gave a low whistle. "And if Phil was murdered in a botched robbery, she'd get everything. Unless she'd hired the killer, in which case she'd still get nothing. Why take the risk?"

"Because Candy hadn't been caught yet," I reminded him. "I doubt Yolanda's last stint in the hospital was the first time Candy approached her about leaving Phil, or getting rid of her problem. We need to talk to Carl before he lawyers up."

He grabbed my upper arm and dragged me to the cruiser where Carson chatted with the other two officers. Carl sat in the back seat, head bowed and hat nowhere in sight. His blond hair was disheveled and sweaty.

"What's going on?" Carson asked.

"We need to talk to Carl," I pushed past him and reached for the door handle.

He stepped in front of me quicker than I expected. "Uh-uh, Dash. No talking to the suspect."

Rob gave him a quick recap of what I'd told him moments ago before pointing to the door. "Can you open it, please?"

Carl squinted. He seemed even more confused than the officers. "What's going on? I thought we were going to the station."

"You are," I told him. "But first, I have one question. Did Yolanda Turner pay you to kill her husband?"

He lowered his gaze to the floor of the cruiser. "Not everyone can pay, but they all want help."

I took his chin in my good hand and gazed directly into his eyes. "She can, and I'm willing to bet anything that she did. Either her or her boyfriend." When Carl flinched, I grinned. "Just say yes or no and we'll take care of the rest."

"Could I have my shoes back until we get to the station?" he pleaded.

Carson chuckled. "Not a chance."

"You took his shoes?" I asked.

Rob shook his head. "They're considered weapons. If you're good, we might let you wear them to walk inside to get your picture taken."

"That's not protocol," Officer Carson groaned.

"Do you mind?" I asked. "We're trying to get his co-operation to catch the people who hired him. I think we can give him an inch of leeway for that, don't you?" Carson scowled. "We'll discuss this later."

Carl smiled. "Thanks, Dash. For the record, Yolanda Turner paid me fifty-thousand dollars to get rid of her husband. Her boyfriend, that goon of Phil's, brought him to the ATM machine we'd agreed on ahead of time, then ducked into the convenience store next door while I conducted business."

"You didn't conduct business," I reminded him. "You killed a man."

Carl shrugged. "That is my business."

I met Rob's gaze. "Is that enough to arrest her Yolanda and Gerald?"

"It's good enough to bring them in for questioning until we get a warrant," he said with a grin. "You wanna ride shotgun?"

"Definitely. I don't want to miss this one," I told them. And I certainly didn't want to have to ride my moped back out there.

Officer Carson threw his hands in the air and grumbled, "Great. So now we're just going to throw all the rules out the window. What next?"

I patted his shoulder. "Next, we pick up the bad guys and you get all the credit. I get to go home and never have to deal with Phil Turner again."

"I'm good with that." He shut the door.

Carl bowed his head and deflated like he'd run out of steam.

"We'd better get moving before they decide to skip town," Rob said.

"We should be safe for a couple hours. She was getting drunk when I left."

Fate was with us, or maybe it was Phil's ghost seeking vengeance. We discovered Yolanda and Gerald lounging by the pool with drinks in hand. The grieving widow had even washed off her make up for the occasion. Not a trace of her late husband's handiwork remained despite her hospital stay.

"We just wanted to make sure you were okay," I told her. "Oh, and to let you know we caught Candy, so she won't bother you anymore."

Yolanda's expression wavered between fear, loathing, and excitement. Not an easy combination to juggle at once. "That's good, right? Now this nightmare will be over."

Rob placed a hand on Gerald's shoulder before he could get off his chair. "That's the interesting part. It seems Carl, or Candy, has a slightly different version of things than you both do."

"What do you mean?" Gerald suddenly seemed tense.

Yolanda reached for her towel. "They're convinced Carl didn't act alone. If they had anything on either of us, they'd have an arrest warrant. Wouldn't they?"

"It's in the works," Rob said. "We're just here to make sure you don't leave town before it arrives. In the meantime, if you'd like to clear the air, I suggest we all take a trip to the police station and have a chat."

She shook her head. "The media will be outraged you're trying to pin my husband's murder on me. I have copies of the hospital records from every time Phil beat me. I'll get nothing but sympathy."

"And life in prison for hiring a hitman." I strolled toward her. If she made a run for it, I'd have no choice but to tackle her into the pool. Cast or not.

Gerald raised his hands in the air. "Cuff me. I'm the guilty one. I've spent years lying to Phil about my relationship with his wife. I deserve to be locked up."

Yolanda stomped her foot. "What happened to 'We're in this together, baby'?"

Rob eased Gerald to his feet and slapped on the handcuffs. "I like this version better. Crimes are solved and nobody got hurt."

She blinked rapidly and grabbed her cell phone. "Except my husband, who's dead. I'm going calling my lawyer. This is harassment."

"And this is assault." I pushed her into the pool as she stormed past me. Yolanda and her phone sank to the bottom, but only she bobbed back up.

"Now that we're clear on all the crimes committed, I just want you to know she's not getting into my car soaking wet," Rob said.

"Can we strap her to the roof?" I asked.

He cringed. "That would be worse than the assault."

"I'll get more towels."

***

Turned out Rob and I had a lot in common. We both preferred beer to margaritas, hockey to football, and loved the thrill of the hunt when it came to our jobs. We'd also both been burned badly in the relationship department and, after three drinks at the bar, spent the rest of the night talking on the beach until the sun came up.

I'd seen a lot more sunsets than sunrises lately. I'm sure it would've been more romantic if we hadn't discussed weapons and cases we'd solved but to each their own.

Good news is, I'm seeing him again Friday.

Bad news was I'll have to go shopping. I need something to wear while I ride on the back of his motorcycle. Shorts and flip-flops won't cut it.

Not where we're going.

-The End-

SON OF A WITCH

DIANE BATOR

DASH ALLMAN MYSTERIES 3

Son of a Witch
Dash Allman PI, Book 3

Diane Bator

Escape With a Writer Publishing

"A girl can never be too careful," I said aloud as I locked my front door behind me. I've had break-ins before, even though the most expensive thing I owned was the phone in my back pocket.

Wiggling my foot a little further into my flip-flop, I pressed one earbud in to listen to Jimmy Buffett crooning about cheeseburgers while my stomach growled in response. I put in the second earbud on my way toward the street. Destination: Ricardo's Food Truck on the beach for the breakfast dog I'd dreamed about last night. Cheese, hot dog, a hashbrown, tomato, bacon, and a fried egg, over easy.

"Watch out for the witch!" a kid yelled.

I huffed, tossing my humidity teased hair. "Okay, it was a rough night, but I don't look that bad."

Just as I reached the sidewalk that stretched before my beach front cottage, someone knocked me over. Bowled me over would be more accurate. I flew in the air like a pin and landed on my butt on the concrete. My left hand smacked the ground hard enough to send twinkling stars drifting around my head.

"Seriously?" I screeched, cradling my wrist in my right hand. Hoping I hadn't broken it for the second time in four months, I looked up to get the license plate of whatever just hit me.

Through twinkling vision, it did look like a bowling ball. Black robes billowed over black tights, and bright rollerblades. A pink-haired witch despite the missing broom. I looked around to see if there was a mob chasing her with pitchforks or if she was just being...well...a witch.

No townsfolk or pitchforks, just a couple neighborhood cops walking quickly toward me. My buddies Officers Alex Carson and Athletic, aka Rob Gwynn as I'd come to know him. We'd been dating off and on over the past three months.

"Mornin'." I got to my feet as gracefully as a three-legged dog. Don't judge me. I had one as a kid.

"Morning, Dash." Carson puffed, moving at a brisk pace. Sweat trickled over his red cheeks and dripped onto his pale blue shirt.

Rob gave a nod. He had yet to break a sweat in spite of matching his partner's pace. "Hey, Dash, how's it going?"

Brushing sand off my legs, I followed them as close as I dared. "When did you guys take up speed walking?"

"Chasing a witch," Carson pointed up the beach.

"You mean the one with pink hair who ran me over?" I asked, as Jimmy Buffett changed tunes to sing about Juicy Fruit. My mouth watered and my stomach rumbled again. I hoped he was almost out of food related songs.

Rob nodded. "That's the one." "Don't you have anything better to do than follow us?"

I adjusted my crooked sunglasses. "Not really. Just heading to Ricardo's for lunch then picking up Halloween candy, so my house doesn't get egged tonight. Don't you have a faster way to chase her? I'm thinking a car might not give my buddy Alex a heart attack."

Carson turned to face me, placing his hands on his hips as he glared. "For the seventh time this month, I'm on a diet.. Stop with the heart attack stuff. My heart is fine."

As I opened my mouth to make a witty comeback, Rob called back from ten feet ahead of us, "Am I going after her alone, or what?"

Carson and I exchanged glances before we hustled to catch up.

"What did the witch do?" I asked.

Rob raised his eyebrows. "Weren't you going to run errands or something?"

My mouth fell open. "Hey, she hit and ran me. I have a stake in this."

"Mmm. Steak would be good," Carson mused. "Maybe I should pick some up after work."

"Focus," Rob snapped. "There've been a series of thefts at the skate park over the past few months. Someone identified the pink-haired girl as a possible suspect. We've been trying to question her, but—"

"But she has wheels, and you have Carson."

"Stop that!" he growled.

I scowled. "I'm not the one who let myself go."

Alex Carson shoved his face into mine. "You just wait until you're my age, young lady. With all of the junk you eat, you're going to look just like me."

Rob nodded. "Exactly."

"You're not helping," I told him.

Up ahead, the pink-haired witch stopped to adjust something beneath her robe. Seizing the opportunity, I darted between the cops, then dodged seniors out for a late morning meander and moms jogging with their babies in strollers.

Rob shouted at me to stop, which alerted the witch. Just as she turned and looked up, I tackled her to the sidewalk. We hit the ground with loud grunts. My knees took the brunt of my fall as her hat sailed past me and landed six feet away. It took a couple seconds before she began to claw at me with coffin-shaped fingernails that matched her pink hair.

"What do you think you're doing?" Officer Athletic—I doubted we'd remain on first name terms after this—hauled me to my feet.

Carson helped the witch to her rollerblades, then snapped a pair of cuffs on her. After that, he checked to make sure she wasn't going to bleed to death in their cruiser from Dash inflicted injuries.

"What are you doing?" she yelled. "Police brutality! You only cuffed me because I'm a witch. That's discrimination. I'll sue."

Athletic held up the hand he didn't have a death grip on my bicep with. "You're a suspect in a crime. We're taking you in for questioning."

She flared her nostrils. "You coulda told me that."

"We did," Carson panted. "Six blocks ago at the skate park."

A little of the fight drained out of her. "I didn't do nothing."

"You didn't do anything," I corrected her.

"See, she gets it." The witch flashed a grin, then narrowed her eyes. "Hey, I know you. You're that P.I. who keeps snooping around the park. Don't you have nothing better to do?"

"Why does everyone keep asking me that?"

Officer Athletic sighed. "Dash, we discussed this."

"And I told you I was on a case," I reminded him.

The witch struggled against her cuffs. "You broke Tommy's leg."

Sanity left the building as Attitude took over. "Oh, yeah? Well, he broke my wrist."

"I knew I shoulda put a curse on you."

Planting my hands on my hips, I retorted, "Joke's on you, Witchy-Poo, I'm already cursed."

"Yeah, that's telling her, Dash," Carson said, then burst into laughter.

Officer Athletic snapped a set of handcuffs onto my wrists as well, and told her, "I can attest to that. I think you should both come for a ride while we clear this up."

I sputtered. "What are you...? I didn't do anything."

"She assaulted me. I got witnesses and I wanna press charges."

Narrowing my eyes, I scowled. "You hit and ran me."

Carson chuckled. "Maybe I'll pick those steaks up on the way back to the station and clock out early today. These two are going to give me a migraine."

"Forget it, Carson." Athletic shook his head. "If I have to deal with them, so do you."

He grinned. "Rob, I've been dealing with Dash for twenty years. It's your turn, now."

* * *

The interrogation room seemed smaller than I remembered. Last time I was in it, I got busted trying to sneak into a suspect's house. They called it Break and Enter, but I was only trying to rescue a mounted swordfish the creep had stolen from my client. Nothing but the best clients for Dash Allman. Anyway, the swordfish in question went for a ride in a cruiser, which helped because I couldn't have carried it to my home office alone and hauling it on my moped wasn't an option.

While the swordfish awaited in an evidence locker, I had sat in that very interrogation room for about six hours before my client made an appearance. When he had the nerved to ask for his deposit back, I refused. That was when someone discovered a hidden compartment in the fish that contained powdery white contraband.

I got off the hook with a stern warning.

My client got ten years and stiffed me.

When the door opened, Officer Athletic appeared with two coffee cups and a wry grin. "Reliving old times?"

"The swordfish." I nodded.

"Of course." He set a cup in front of me before taking a seat across the metal table and releasing a sigh that made me feel completely guilty.

I held up my bound wrists. "Can you at least remove these?"

He took his sweet time reaching into his pocket and sorting through dozens of keys before he unlocked the cuffs. He was smart enough to put them away before I did anything else stupid.

"You know I had to do that," he told me. "She was making a scene, and you do have a bit of a reputation."

"At least I enjoyed her rant all the way here about how I broke Tommy Vale's leg for no reason and that he's going to sue me." I sipped my coffee, then straightened my back in surprise. "Mm. This isn't cop shop coffee."

Rob shrugged. "I may have needed to walk off a bit of frustration, so I went up the beach to Mayberry."

Yup. Back to first names after he got me the good stuff.

Over the past three months, Mayberry Café had become one of our favorite places to meet for lunch. It was also a convenient location to meet with potential clients and blackmailers. Away from my home office and close to the police station. But not too close.

"That was sweet," I said, fluffing my hair as I smiled. "Were you frustrated thinking about me in handcuffs, or…"

"Or because you tend to act first and think about consequences later?" He hesitated, then grinned. "A bit of both, actually."

Fairly sure both our faces were red, I focused on my coffee until a thought struck me. "Did the witch confess to the thefts?"

His shoulders sagged when he released an even deeper sigh. "No, but she did mutter a curse or two with your name in them. We didn't find anything on her either. Just her wallet and a little bag of crystals."

"Meth?"

He shook his head. "The sparkly rock kind."

"You mean crystals, as in quartz and amethyst?"

"Actually, Swarovski. For making jewelry and stuff."

I whistled. "Fancy. Did you talk to Tommy Vale?"

"Boy, did I," Rob said. "When he came to pick her up, I caught an earful about how he was going to sue us for harassing her."

"Good thing I was in here the whole time."

"Oh, don't worry. When he finds you, he's going to teach you not to accuse him of crimes he didn't commit. Care to explain that one?"

Nope. I definitely didn't. "Of course, he threatened me, which is why I'm still here. Protective custody, right?"

Rob smirked. "Actually, you're still here because I lost the coin toss. Forty-nine times out of fifty."

My eyes widened. "Fifty?"

"Neither me nor Alex wanted to come in and officially tell you to back off the skate park case," he admitted.

"Officially?"

When he winced, little lines radiated from his left eye as it twitched a couple times. "Unofficially, since you're taking the heat off us, the thieves might slip up while trying to avoid you."

I hugged my coffee cup with both hands and sat back to think. "So, you're using me as a decoy."

Rob shrugged at first, then said, "In a manner of speaking, yes."

"Do I get paid for this?"

"You get out of interrogation for free."

"Even though the witch assaulted me first."

Rob rubbed both eyes with one hand. "How about if I take you out for dinner after work tonight?"

"Lunch would be better," I told him. "I missed breakfast, thanks to that little witch. Nowhere fancy though. I skinned both my knees when I tackled her. I could use a few bandages if you've got some handy. What was her name, anyway?"

"Patience Dogood."

I chuckled. "Now there's a witchy name if I ever heard one."

* * *

Lunch was ultra casual. After we grabbed a backpack from the trunk of Rob's car, we ordered breakfast dogs and fries from Ricardo's, then sat on a hill near the skatepark looking for trouble. Well, signs of trouble, anyway.

"I hope this is okay." Rob said, pausing to sip his milkshake. "You did say nowhere fancy."

I grinned, sucking ketchup off my fingers. "I did. Me and my skinned knees fit in better here than at Christo's or somewhere like that."

He pointed to a couple kids on a halfpipe. "Actually, pretty much everyone here is smart enough to wear kneepads and helmets."

"Just my luck I left home without protection today." When he raised his eyebrows, I rolled my eyes. "You know what I mean."

"Lucky for you."

As I slurped the last of my mocha milkshake, I noticed two people approach the park from the far end. "There's Tommy."

"That's not Patience with him though," Rob said, holding up his cell phone to snap a picture. "She didn't have enough time to dye her hair blue."

"Glinda. His sister. She was here the day I tried to take down Tommy and everything went bad. I think she's the one who called the ambulance."

He raised his eyebrows. "You think?"

I held up my left hand. "Broken wrist, remember? I was a little distracted. You want me to go talk to them?"

"Nope. I want you to stay right here." Rob reached into the backpack. As he pulled out a skateboard and protective gear, he ignored my gawking, then suited up and walked down the hill.

"That man's crazier than I thought."

That man was also amazing on a skateboard. I watched—and videoed—in awe as he did tricks I'd only seen one or two diehards around the park pull off. It wasn't just to impress me, either. Rob Gwynn knew his stuff.

Once Rob stopped to adjust his helmet, Tommy made his move. Although I itched to get closer to hear, I kept my distance as ordered. I didn't want to spook our suspect, or his sister who lurked in the shadows looking pouty.

Before long, the two men shared a good laugh, then hopped on their boards. I hated feeling left out, but I already had that card in my wallet the nurses made me at the hospital. It was supposed to work as reverse psychology, but one more broken bone this year and I'd get a free hot dog at Ricardo's.

"What are you doing here?" a woman asked. "I thought you'd be home in your rocking chair getting ready to hand out candy."

I scowled at Patience before turning my gaze back to Rob and Tommy. The thought of being nice fluttered through my head. I ignored it. "Thanks to you, I haven't been able to get to the store yet. I'll end up with eggs and toilet paper all over the house later."

Uninvited, she sat next to me on the grass. "Doubt it. After the whole Covid thing, no one does toilet paper anymore. Eggs are fair game though."

"What are you doing here, Patience?" I asked, not wanting to acknowledge that she had a point.

"The cute cop told you my name, huh? Not like I care. I came to watch Tommy. I didn't expect the Wicked Witch to be hanging out though."

"Glinda?" Why did that name ring a bell? Ah. Wizard of Oz. Although in that story, Glinda was the good witch.

Patience leaned closer and whispered, "You know how Tommy tells everyone she's his sister?"

"Yeah," I replied slowly, wary of every word that came from her mouth.

"She's his sister like I can make pigs fly."

I offered her a limp french fry. "So, you're trying to catch them in the act?"

"They stole my board," Patience said. "I came to get back what's mine."

She pulled out her phone and swiped until she found a picture of a pink skateboard decorated with a black witch riding her own skateboard. "That witch is done in Swarovski crystals. She's one of a kind and cost me over six hundred bucks."

I whistled. "That's a lot of money for a skateboard. What? No broom?"

"Oh, please. Brooms are so sixteen hundreds." Patience tucked a strand of pink hair behind one ear. "That's not just a board. It's a custom street deck designed and handmade by Skull Richardson."

My eyebrow twitched. Skull was the client who'd hired me three months earlier to keep an eye open for stolen boards, and for Tommy Vale. For now, I played dumb and asked, "Should I know who that is?"

She shrugged. "Not if you're not into the scene. He does some wild artwork on decks and has a six-month waiting list. You should Google him."

"I'll do that. Thanks."

"Do you need help to figure that out?" she asked.

I scowled. I wasn't as old as she seemed to think I was. "I'll get by."

Patience got up and started down the hill, then paused a few steps away. She glanced back. "Sorry for the whole hit and run thing. I hate being chased by cops, especially when I didn't do anything. Can you believe they thought my crystals were real diamonds? As if!"

The skin on the back of my neck rippled, but I forced a smile. "Just a tip. Next time, don't run if you didn't do anything."

She grinned. "Huh. Smart thinkin'. Maybe you're not so bad after all."

"Oh, boy." I groaned as she headed to where Tommy and Rob compared boards. When Rob reached into his pocket, I muttered, "Don't give him your card. Don't give him your card."

Too late. Rob handed Tommy what looked like his business card before turning to jog back up the hill. So much for any chance to go undercover. Tommy seemed to meet my gaze across the field between us and scowled before joining Glinda. Together, they strolled toward a bright yellow convertible.

Pulling out my phone, I did a little surfing even though I already knew Skull Richardson was a former pro skateboarder around thirty, who'd suffered a couple career ending crashes ten years earlier. The broken shoulder he could've come back from, according to the experts, but the coma and severe concussion ground his wheels to a stop.

Patience was right about Skull's custom boards. Not only were they works of art made completely by hand for each client they cost far more than your average store-bought board—or monthly rent. Some he'd adorned with crystals, like the one for Patience. Others were handmade with intricately carved exotic woods.

"Geez, those aren't skateboards," I said aloud, "they're works of art."

"What are?" Rob collapsed onto the grass next to me with a loud moan. After squirming on the grass for a couple seconds, he lay on his back.

"You ever hear of Skull Richardson?"

His eyes grew wide. "Of course. I used to skate with him back in the day. Tommy just mentioned Skull's custom boards and designs. It seems like most of the boards stolen over the past few months were ones Skull made for the locals."

"Skull's the one who hired me this summer, and why I keep hanging around the skate park. I think we should stop by his shop after I get candy."

"Candy?"

"Halloween?"

Rob groaned. "Right. Do you think Skull knows why his boards are being targeted?

"I'll bet you a box of donuts he does."

He bent his left arm to hold up a fist. "You're on."

Bumping his fist with mine, I got up. "You want to drop by his shop now or tomorrow?"

"Tomorrow." Rob didn't move.

I waited a few long seconds before asking, "Are you okay?"

"I tweaked my back doing that last jump. A little help?"

* * *

Rob shuffled beside me as we went back to my place for ice. Skull's shop was two blocks from my house and, for once, I had ice in the freezer. I'd learned the hard way after my last fracture.

"How's your back?" I asked.

"If I don't sit, breath, or sneeze, it's great."

I chuckled. "So, the skateboarding thing was a brief chance to relive your teen years and you're over it?"

He muttered as he led the way down the sidewalk. Five seconds later, he lay flat on his back next to someone dressed as a witch with blue hair. Both writhed in pain. Looked like I'd be on my own talking to Skull once I got Rob to a couch.

"Sorry, dude," Blue Hair said, hopping to their feet and starting to skate away.

"Not so fast, Glinda." I lunged over Rob to grab the only part of the skateboarder I could reach. A wig and pointy hat came off in my hand.

"You're not Glinda," I told the lean, blond surfer dude as we gawked at each other. His pupils were much more dilated than mine. Drugs?

He growled, snatching back the wig. "Give that back. Geez, lady, you're gonna blow my cover."

By then, Rob had rolled to his side and threatened to cuff the guy.

"Yeah? I'm shaking, pops," he said. "You can't even get up."

I scowled. "Well, stop shaking and help me get him up."

"He's yours?"

"It's only been a couple months. We haven't gotten that far," I said.

Rob snarled as we helped him to his feet. "I ought to cuff you both just on principle."

Surfer Dude chuckled. "You'd have to catch us first."

I chuckled. "Don't encourage him. He threw out his back at the skatepark and you might've just broken him."

"Bummer. Hey, that was you? Dude, you were good."

I smirked as Rob limped between us to my front door. "Since you're obviously not Glinda, who are you and how do you know Tommy Vale?"

Surfer Dude shook his head. "I don't hafta tell you nothing."

"Geez, don't they teach English in school anymore?" I reached behind Rob to smack the kid in the head. "Answer the question while you help me get him to my couch."

"You live here?" Surfer Dude asked. "Sweet pad."

I unlocked the door, let us all inside, then we helped Rob to the couch. "Thanks. Now, tell me who you are."

"You're not a cop." He folded his arms across his skinny chest.

"No, but he is."

Surfer Dude paled. "Oh. He's not gonna arrest me, is he?"

"No, but if you don't answer our questions, I might shoot you," Rob said, easing onto his back. "Who are you and what's your relationship to Tommy?"

Surfer Dude tucked a couple pillows behind Rob's back while I grabbed the painkillers I kept on hand for the same reason as the ice. I seemed to have a need for both on a regular basis.

"Glinda's my stage name. I'm a drag queen."

Rob's eyes bugged. "You're a what?"

I handed him a glass of water and two pills. "Take these. Sorry, buddy, but you don't look like a drag queen."

Glinda took out his phone and pulled up a website that showed before, during, and after shots of his process from Surfer Dude to Glinda Mae Witch.

"Get it?" he said. "It's a play on Glinda the Good Witch and Mae West. My parents are witches, so..."

I started to sit, then remembered I still had to get candy and go to Skull's shop. "Are you going to be okay here alone, Rob?"

"I'm coming with you." He tried to move, then gasped and stopped. "Maybe I'll wait here."

Patting his shoulder, I agreed. "The meds will kick in soon. I don't want you falling on your face while I'm deciding which chocolate bars to get."

"I like chocolate," Glinda announced.

"Good to know." Locking the door, my new sidekick and I walked to the grocery store a block away to scoop the last two bags of mini chocolate bars. By the time we'd reached Skull's shop five minutes later, we'd eaten half the first bag.

Skull wasn't as impressive as his name implied. A thin, pale, thirty-something year old, he'd developed hunched shoulders from his work. He looked more like Quasimodo than the lean, tanned athlete he used to be.

"Did you catch 'em?" he asked. "Is that the thief?"

"Hey, Skull," Glinda said around a mouthful of chocolate.

Skull squinted. "Oh. It's you. Dash, you'd better have good news for me. Whoever's stealing my boards is trashing my rep. Kids have cancelled orders because they don't want to lose their investment."

I frowned. "That's ridiculous."

Glinda poked around the shop as though looking for something.

Skull kept an eye on him before he grabbed a plain deck from Glinda's hands. "I think you two should leave."

My P.I. senses squirming, I told Glinda I'd see him later.

"But I—" he started, gaze on the shopping bag that held the chocolate.

Shaking my head, I pointed to the door. "Out."

The last thing I wanted was for the witch to further aggravate my client, which was exactly the road we were going down. I also didn't want him to be taking my chocolate. Once Glinda was gone, Skull closed and locked the door.

"I take it you two don't get along."

Skull stood so close I could smell tuna on his breath and see the small blackheads that dotted his nose. I took a quick glance around for anything I could hurt him with if needed. "Glinda the Naughty Witch is my competition."

"Are you sure?"

He rolled his eyes. "What kind of P.I. are you? He and Tommy work out of a shop on Holyrood. Their decks aren't the same quality as mine, but I wouldn't put it past them to steal mine to drum me out of business."

Why hadn't he shared that tidbit with me three months ago before I started stalking kids at the park? I agreed with Skull, how had I missed finding that out earlier? I decided to blame it on the broken wrist.

"They're definitely suspects. What about customers? Has anyone bought a deck or wanted one designed, then refused to pay for it?"

"Never," he said. "Although I did have one chick say her board was stolen right after she got it and she wanted her money back. Not the smartest banana in the bunch. I explained that wasn't how life worked and sent her on her way. She got mad and swore she'd get even. Not sure for what since I sold her what she wanted."

My neck tingled. "Do you remember what her board looked like?"

Skull pointed to the far wall. "I'll go you one better. I take pictures of every board I make and post it there. Sometimes with their new owners."

I wasn't surprised when he tapped the shiny photo of a pink, Swarovski crystal covered board with a black witch. "Patience."

"Forget it." He snorted. "I'm running outta patience. You need to catch the creeps before they run me out of town."

"No, that's the girl's name. Patience Dogood."

"The pink-haired kid? Nah. That's Abigail Vale. She's Tommy's stepsister."

My eyes widened. "You sure she's not his girlfriend?"

He laughed. "Dude, you're funny. Tommy's gay. He and that Glinda kid hooked up years ago."

Suddenly, I needed to find Patience Dogood, aka Abigail Vale. First, I had to make amends to Skull by offering the only thing I could. "Chocolate?"

"Don't mind if I do." He happily took the rest of the half-empty bag.

* * *

I peeked in on Rob before heading back to the skate park. He snored so loudly I closed the door and went back outside for some peace. Maybe he wasn't the man of my dreams after all. Or maybe it was the sleeping pills I gave him. At least his back didn't seem to be bothering him for the moment.

Patience rolled back and forth across a flat area on the park on a plain, pink skateboard. No tricks or showing off, she'd simply push off and glide from one wall to the other. Weird form of pacing if you asked me.

"We need to talk." I caught up to her. "It's about Tommy."

She dropped a foot to the ground and stopped to stare. "Is he okay? I haven't seen him since you were here earlier."

"What happened to your witch skateboard?" I asked.

Her face flushed. "I was stolen, like I said."

"Who stole it?"

"How should I know?"

"Did you leave it somewhere or did someone jump you?" I asked.

No reply.

The next time she pushed off to roll away, I put my foot on the front of her board. "Let's try a different approach. Why are you helping your stepbrother steal boards, Abigail?"

The red in her cheeks melted away as she paled. Tears welled in her eyes. I released her board out of pity before she started talking, "Tommy and Glinda, whose real name is Chip by the way, got this bright idea they could do better designs than Skull. Only they couldn't. They got pictures from an AI program that always had glitches. Not to mention, Skull's got talent. He makes his own boards from bits of wood. His decks are perfect. T and C bought cheap ones wholesale from overseas and glue on cheesy designs."

"But people didn't want to pay big bucks for poor quality."

"Exactly." She stopped at the wall, turned, and pushed off to go in the other direction.

"T and C. Is that the name of their company?"

Patience nodded. "Yeah. Tommy's also Chip's, I mean, Glinda's manager. She's a drag performer."

"And since they're a couple, you never stood a chance to be your stepbrother's girlfriend, did you?"

"It sounds silly, right?" She sighed. "I've had a crush on Tommy since we were in first grade. We coulda had a chance but our parents met and got married two years ago. It's hard to get over all that."

"Are you the one stealing skateboards to help Tommy and Glinda?"

She stopped to look me in the eye. "No. I came up with the idea one night while we were partying, but I never stole anything."

"Then who did?"

She looked around to make sure we were alone before she answered, "My brother."

"Tommy?" I asked. "Then I was right all along."

"No, it was Chip."

If I thought I'd had the whole mess sorted out before, suddenly things were as clear as a milkshake. "Wait a sec. Chip's your brother, Tommy's your stepbrother, and the two of them are dating even though your parents are married. Wow. I thought my family was messed up." I paused for a breath. "Can you help me find Chip? I have a lot more questions for him than I thought."

Patience took another glance around us. "Maybe we should bring your cop friend along. We might need backup."

"We could, but we'd probably have to carry him." I pulled out my phone.

Officer Alex Carson would be mad I bothered him, especially after he'd bought steaks, but we could get two thieves off the streets and close a case that nagged us both. I hit speed dial, explained the situation between Pasty's outbursts, then gave him the address for T and C Board Shop. He must've been at the grocery store getting steak because he arrived in a blue convertible before we'd even rounded the corner.

"This better be good, Dash," he muttered.

"Trust me. This will be worth it."

Patience nodded, pushing open the front door of the shop. The scents of glue and reefer assaulted us as she called out, "Hey, guys. I have a new customer for you."

Tommy emerged from the back room wiping his hands with a red cloth. "How can I help... Oh, crap. Not you again."

Carson took a step forward but didn't get a chance to speak before Glinda, aka Chip, appeared. With a quick glance at the three of us, he spun around and bolted.

"I hate this part," I muttered as I pushed past Patience and Tommy, then raced after the surfer dude.

Considering his cardio was a hundred times better than mine, I had to outsmart him before he reached the door. I grabbed a couple loose wheels as I ran past a table and threw them at the back of his head. His aim was probably a hundred times better than mine, too. Both wheels missed.

Although, I got lucky when one deflected off the steel door and hit him in the face.

"Son of a...," he yelled before doubling over.

By the time I reached him, blood gushed everywhere. I grabbed a blue cloth off a nearby rack and held it to his face. Within seconds, he passed out.

"What did you do to him?" Carson asked, as he marched into the room with both Tommy and Patience in handcuffs. I'd underestimated him.

I explained the wheel, the door, and the nose, then held up the now purple rag. "I tried to stop the bleeding, but he passed out."

"Dude," Tommy said, his chin quivering as though he was torn between laughing and crying. "Blue is for glue."

I sniffed the rag and got an instant buzz.

***

"Trick or treat," a tiny dragon shouted in our direction.

I threw a chocolate bar at it.

"Don't be so mean," Rob said. "How's the kid supposed to find it with that big, stuffed tail knocking it away when he turns around?"

"Next year he should get a better costume."

The dragon's mother rushed to its aid and threw me a scowl.

Rob handed her a second chocolate bar. Once they left, he chuckled. "You're lucky Alex made us both dinner after all the trouble you caused today."

"Yeah, I'm lucky to sit on his porch handing out candy instead of keeping my house from getting egged because I shut down T and C."

He shrugged. "They were stealing boards and shipping them out of state. Tommy and Chip will get time to think things over and Patience will be grounded until she's fifty. Skull's business will boom again until the next board shop opens. Even better, I got a great sleep and my back feels amazing. It all worked out."

"I suppose." I peeled open a mini chocolate bar and settled back to enjoy the balmy air, the full moon, and the scent of steaks sizzling in the backyard. My stomach grumbled as Jimmy Buffett sang over Pasty's speakers about fruitcakes. He couldn't have been more right.

"I still can't believe you drugged Chip," Carson said as he emerged from the house carrying three beers.

"How was I supposed to know they used the blue rags and solvent to clean excess glue off the boards?" I asked. "I guarantee I'll hear 'blue is for glue' in my sleep for weeks."

Both men laughed, then sipped their drinks before Carson added, "At least I got the creeps off the streets."

"Excuse me?"

He met my gaze. "Were you planning to haul the three of them to the station on your moped?"

"Good point," I mumbled. "Thanks, Alex."

His jaw dropped as he cupped one ear. "What?"

Darn. He was going to make me say it again. "I said thanks, Alex."

Alex Carson grinned wider than the jack-o-lantern on his front porch. "Best treat ever. Anyone ready for steak?"

"Do I get out of candy duty?" I asked.

"Just leave the bowl on the porch before you take out some kid's eye."

I stared. "You mean we could've just done that from the start?"

"Yup. But it was a lot more entertaining watching you throw candy at the kids and tick off the parents."

It was my turn to grin. "At least they don't know where I live."

"No," Alex said, "but I do."

As he walked away cackling, Jimmy Buffett sang about gypsies in the palace. I had half a mind to run home and check on my house, but the scent of grilled steak…

My stomach rumbled.

-The End-

VISIONS OF GUMDROP

DIANE BATOR

ASH ALLMAN MYSTERIES BOOK 4

Visions of Gumdrop

Dash Allman PI, Book 4

Diane Bator

Escape With a Writer Publishing

Jimmy Buffett had just started crooning about Christmas in Hawaii when I got a text urging me to *"Stay indoors until further notice. Escaped animal on the loose."*

My stomach lurched as I shot a quick reply to the sender, my on-again off-again boyfriend, Rob Gwynn who was a local police officer. *"What kind of animal?"*

I didn't wait for a reply. It was the last Saturday morning before Christmas and the local market would be in full swing in fifteen minutes. No way was I missing it. I had shopping to do. Besides, no one would be dumb enough to transport a dangerous creature this close to a populated beach, would they?

I opened my front door anyway.

After looking both ways for large, furry beasts and witches on rollerblades, I stepped into the sunshine and locked the front door of my beach cottage-slash-office. Ever since I was a kid, I've been a curious cat, which made me an ideal detective. Not the best one money could buy, but definitely in the top one hundred on the coast.

Definitely, the only one with the oddball name of Dash.

The joke in my family was that my mom fell in love with Dashiell Hammett at first sight, which made childhood rough for the little girl she named Dashiell Allman. Not funny. Although, the nickname Dash did make me feel faster when I ran. Potential clients tended to call me out of curiosity since my name made me sound like a strong, male detective.

Once they met me in person—a short, blonde, beach bum usually sporting a cast of some sort—some ran. Most laughed. A few took pity on me and hired me on a trial basis.

Crossing the beach, I aimed for the wet sand where the waves could caress my toes on my way to Ricardo's food truck. I woke up craving a breakfast dog and my growling stomach finally got the best of me as I'd finished the paperwork from my last case. Visions of a hot dog, cheese a hashbrown, tomato, bacon, and a fried egg over easy had danced through my head for the past hour.

The air was a bit cooler than earlier in December. A reminder that I still needed to pick up gifts for my two favorite police officers. Rob Gwynn, aka Officer Athletic and my current boyfriend, was big into action movies, working out, and muscle cars. I had no idea what to get him.

Alex Carson, his partner and the man I'd called Officer Alex for years, was easier. He was a foodie who loved to cook. A couple of weeks ago, I'd discovered a great booth at the market that sold homemade spices and rubs. I'd finally decided which ones to get him and planned to hit the market. Right after breakfast.

Something wet brushed against the back of my right shoulder. I brushed it off like a bug. Then it tapped me again.

"Very funny, Rob," I said, stopping to turn around. "What the...?"

I came face to face with an elongated nose attached to a furry creature that looked like a cross between a horse and a tall sheep. My jaw dropped and my eyes grew wide.

Its nostrils flared before a wad of phlegm hit me square in the chest. Then it yelled "Mwah!" and collapsed into the sand.

"What the flying fig just happened?" I asked, taking a couple steps back.

"What did you do to it, Dash?" a familiar voice asked.

On cue, Rob and Alex loped across the beach, more concerned about the creature than the fact I'd been accosted.

I held up my hands in protest. "Nothing. It just fell over. I don't even know what it is."

"It's a llama, Dash," Alex Carson told me with a chuckle. "Didn't you learn anything in school?"

Scowling at the two-hundred-and-fifty-pound officer, I shook my head. "I've seen pictures of them, but I've never looked one in the nostrils before. What's it doing on the beach?"

Rob looped a rope around its neck, flinching when the llama rolled away from him to sit in the sand. "It's part of the petting zoo at the market today. While the farmer was unloading the animals, this little guy escaped."

"Little? That thing's a full head taller than you and smells like a barnyard."

He grinned and petted the creature like an overgrown dog. "Aww, did the grumpy detective scare you, Gumdrop?"

"Ha. The grumpy detective nearly peed her pants." I took one last look at the llama. If I were a social media-type person, I would've taken pictures. No one in my family would believe I came face to face with a llama, let alone one that fainted on the spot.

For everyone else, it wouldn't be much of a surprise.

As Gumdrop rose to its cloven feet, I backed away. "Seems like you two have this well in hand. I'm going for breakfast."

"Let me guess," Rob said. "A breakfast dog?"

"You got it."

Alex groaned. "Oh, Dash, those things are heart attacks on a bun. You need to stay away from them."

"Maybe, but they're tasty and will keep me going all day." Turning away, I continued up the beach only to hear a commotion behind me. I refused to go back. They were on their own with the stinky, shaggy beast.

"Look out, Dash!" Alex shouted.

I spun around in the sand only to wind up nose to nose with Gumdrop once more. It spit at me again. The llama had good aim. Loogie number two landed right beside the first one.

"Seriously?" I yelled.

Gumdrop dropped to the sand.

I pointed to the drama llama. "See. That's what happened the first time."

Before Rob could take hold of the rope dangling from the creature's neck, a group of men strode toward us. Two more police officers. A man in an elf costume. A thin guy wearing jeans, a red nose, and a plaid shirt. A large Santa whose padding had shifted to the right of his belly. Bringing up the rear was a man in denim overalls and a torn t-shirt, likely the farmer.

"Oh. goodie. Backup. Have fun. I'm outta here." I announced as the llama sat up and spit at me again.

Shaking my head, I aimed for Ricardo's food truck near the pier. Drama llamas were not my thing. With no clients on my schedule, I looked forward to a much-needed day off. And a breakfast dog.

When the first bite of breakfast dog filled my mouth, I forgot all about the spitting llama and the strange scene on the beach. Well, after I had a good chuckle reliving the whole adventure with Ricardo and his wife. At least it made for a great story.

I cleaned the spittle off my shirt using half a bottle of water. Sated and caffeinated from a large coffee, I wandered away from the beach, past the flock of pink flamingoes, wearing Santa hats and strung with lights, that Ricardo had jabbed into the sand, and up the street to the market.

Festive lights hung overhead with timers set to turn them on at dusk. Three-foot Norfolk Island pines filled the dozen or so planters on the sidewalks that usually held flowers and dune grasses. A twenty-foot Daisy spruce stood in front of town hall. Town employees and volunteers had decorated it with LED lights and large, gaudy plastic ornaments.

The Promenade, our main street, was closed to cars for the day, and lined with about sixty small tents and twice as many tables. Christmas was a big deal here. Even if we never saw natural snow.

I picked up the gourmet spices for Alex. A homemade, essential oil weight bench cleaner with a matching shower gel for Rob. A cute little pink flamingo Christmas ornament for my four-foot, fake Christmas tree. A cactus adorned with gumdrop lights and googly eyes that one of my clients had delivered last week.

Gumdrop. I smirked. Who in their right mind named a fainting llama Gumdrop? Apparently, the same guy who owned said fainting llama.

From up the street, I heard "Mwah."

My breath stuck in my throat, and I had half a mind to book it for home. There was, however, one last booth I itched to stop at. The chocolate tent. Weighing the pros and scratching the cons, I went for it. Unfortunately, the chocolate booth was within eyesight of the petting zoo. And the llama. The minute I got close, Gumdrop launched a wad of spit before falling over in a pile of fresh straw.

"You really need to leave him alone," Rob said, falling into step beside me.

Boyfriend or not, I scowled. "Shouldn't you be at work instead of following me?"

"I am at work. We're on a case." He followed me to the chocolate stand. "While we were searching for Gumdrop, someone stole one of Henry's prize Angora goats."

I met his gaze, not sure how to react to the news. "I take it Henry is the farmer. Someone got his goat?"

He rolled his eyes at my sense of humor. "Stole his goat. A Daisy-ribbon Angora worth several thousand dollars."

"They stole a goat?" I asked again. "On purpose?"

"Yes. Stop saying that. I need your help."

"Not a chance." I picked out my chocolate and handed the woman cash. "I'm sorry. This is all just so silly. It's Christmas, not goat and llama season. Find a few shepherds. I'll bet they could round up the goat in no time."

"That's not funny."

"Then call in a little drummer boy." I paused. "Oh. I suppose that's not a politically correct term anymore, is it?"

"Dash…" His face contorted in pain. A look he often had around me. "All I'm asking is for you to keep your eyes and ears open. Chances are, whoever took the goat's long gone, but just in case. Please, humor me."

"Too bad about the chaos at the petting zoo," the woman selling chocolates said. "I love how it brings in the families. Kids and their moms all love chocolate, especially this time of year."

I snorted and grumbled. "Yeah. Animals are great."

Particularly behind bars. Bad enough I didn't like animals on a good day, they didn't seem to like me much either. If the llama was rude enough to spit at me, I had no idea what a goat would do. Even a hoity-toity Daisy-ribbon winning one.

To appease Rob, I meandered toward the petting zoo where Farmer Henry kept watch over the two pens like a vulture. One pen held a couple pigs, a goat, two chickens, a sheep, and a miniature pony. Kids were allowed to feed and pet them but not venture into the pen, which only assured me they were all dangerous. The kids and the creatures.

The second pen held Gumdrop and a black and white spotted cow. Both narrowed their eyes as they watched me and chewed slowly. I'd faced murderers and thieves before. The cow and llama side by side scared me far more. People were much more predictable than animals.

"Hey, you're the one what scared Gumdrop." Farmer Henry said, jabbing a finger against my chest, precisely where the wet goo once sat. "You get my goat?"

I'd been so spooked by the critters that I hadn't noticed him move off his stool. "The police are looking for it. Actually, your drama llama scared me. How did that thing get loose anyway?"

"The thief who stole my goat let her out." He glared at me, then asked, "It wasn't you, was it?"

I shook my head. "Nope. Don't look at me. I don't even like animals."

"Mwah," Gumdrop called out. When he shot a wad of spit, it landed between us on top of a chicken who ran as though the sky was falling.

The farmer sighed. "That missing goat's worth a lot of money. I wasn't going to bring her, but the market organizer insisted. He wanted us to let people take pictures with her and Gumdrop."

I smirked, imagining the llama fainting after each picture. The whole endeavor would've taken until Christmas.

"Who's the organizer?" I asked.

"Everett Collins. Skinny guy wearing a neon green t-shirt and a Santa hat. His wife, Becky, runs the chocolate booth."

Thoughts scrambled through my head like a half dozen marbles turned loose in a pinball machine. "I'll be back in a minute."

"Mwah," Gumdrop yelled, then fell over.

I rolled my eyes. "You need to take that thing to a vet. There's something seriously wrong with it."

"There ain't nothing wrong with him," he told me. "I have a couple goats with myotonia congenita, is all."

"What's that?"

"Vet says it makes their muscles go stiff when they get scared. People call 'em fainting goats. Gumdrop's been in a pen with them since they were all babies and copies 'em. He's healthy as a horse."

I chuckled. "Maybe you should consider putting him in therapy."

"Why? He's happier than a pig in muck."

Rob and Alex stood at the far end of the street chatting with market vendors. No sense in all of us talking to the same people. I ducked behind a row of booths to my left and peered into the windows of trucks and vans parked near stalls. Not every stall had the luxury of close parking, only the produce booths and the petting zoo.

And a white panel furniture truck with the rear door wide open. No goats in sight. Plenty of fabulous hand-carved tables, bowls, and lamps though. I was impressed by the handiwork and did a mental tally of my bank account.

"Can I help you?" a man six inches shorter than me asked.

"Are these yours?"

"Yeah. Why?"

His snarky attitude took me by surprise considering he wore an elf hat and fake pointy ears. I wanted to ask how he'd escaped the North Pole but held my tongue. I'd already offended a llama, why get elves involved?

"I was thinking my parents might like that horse lamp," I told him. "How much is it?"

"For you? Five hundred dollars."

The elf's tone made me bristle. I narrowed my eyes. "And how much for everyone else?"

"A hundred," he said. When I gawked, he grinned. "I know who you are, Dash Allman. You're the PI who got my cousin locked up."

I squinted and took a closer look to see if he resembled anyone I'd collared lately. "Who's your cousin?"

"Victor Chaney."

My fists clenched as if they had tiny minds of their own. Victor was the scum bag who hired me to get back his stuffed swordfish from the man he convinced me stole it.

When I broke into the other man's house to retrieve it, the police arrested me and took me into an interrogation room. The swordfish hung out in evidence. Victor stormed into the station, fired me, and demanded his deposit back. Karma bit him in the backside when one of the officers discovered a powdery white substance stashed inside the fish. As far as I knew, both Victor and the swordfish were still locked up.

"Victor's a creep. He deserved it," I announced.

The elf folded his muscular arms across his barrel chest. "Never said he didn't. I'm just trying to help his wife earn a few grand for his defense."

I shook my head, the fingers of a tension headache clawing their way up the back of my neck. "Keep the horse. That dirt bag still owes me five hundred for that case."

"And you still have his fish."

"No, the police have his fish. And his drugs," I corrected him, then waved a hand. "Forget it. Oh, you haven't seen a stray goat wandering around, have you?"

He looked at me as if I'd grown two more eyes. "A goat? Not since this morning when some clown let the whole barnyard loose."

I glanced at the petting zoo and recalled the man with the red nose I'd seen on the beach. Did he mean a literal clown? "The whole barnyard?"

"Yup. Pigs, goats, cows, chickens.... That stupid llama tried to get into the back of my van. When I yelled at it, the critter fainted."

Stifling my laugh, I replied, "I've heard that's a thing."

The elf placed a hand on one of his tables. "Once they rounded up the animals, I noticed one of my pieces was missing. A lamp with an owl on a tree branch that's worth a couple hundred bones."

First a missing goat, now a wooden owl. I frowned then asked, "Do you have a picture of it?"

He stared at me for a long, agonizing moment. Back at the petting zoo, the llama shouted seconds before people burst out laughing. Gumdrop must've fainted again. Guess it wasn't just my influence after all.

"Here," the elf said, thrusting a piece of paper at me. "I made these for prospective buyers, which you're obviously not." But if you get the owl back, I might give you a discount on the horse. My number's on the bottom."

I studied the image of the clock in question. Below it was his name, Dog Chaney, and a phone number. An elf named Dog. I struggled to hide yet another grin. "Gee, thanks. Did you report the missing clock to the police?"

"Yeah. For all that good that's gonna do. They're focused on the goat."

I walked away before saying anything I'd regret. As I passed the town Christmas tree, someone dressed as Santa with a burgundy suit tuck a small package beneath it. I could've sworn there were only a couple packages under those branches earlier. Now there were about a dozen of all sizes.

Suspicious, I started toward the tree with no idea what to do. Open them? Call for help? Finally, I decided to leave the packages untouched and find Rob or Alex instead. The last thing I wanted was to put my fingerprints all over them if they were evidence.

I ran into Rob at a booth that sold organic wines. He had one bottle in each hand—one red and one alcohol-free. What was the point of that? So much for police work.

"Hey, what's with the Christmas tree?" I asked.

"You've lived here your whole life, Dash," he replied. "You know the town puts up a Christmas tree every year."

Scowling, I put a hand on my hip as I hit him with my shopping bags. "I do know that. But this is the first year I've seen presents under it. Is that a charity thing? You know they're just tempting thieves."

He narrowed his eyes. "Presents? Not that I know of. They would've asked for security. Are you sure?"

"Come with me, Inspector Clueless." I grabbed his arm and led him past several tables. When I pointed to the growing pile of gifts, he reached for his radio and called Alex to bring the organizer to the tree.

"It could just be a charity thing," I offered again.

Alex Carson appeared moments later dragging a man in a bright green shirt behind him and asked, "What's going on?"

Everett Collins met my gaze, his hazel eyes more bloodshot than mine. He seemed to deflate a little. Why did I have that effect on people today? He cleared his throat and tried to sound authoritative when he clutched his green clipboard in front of his stomach and asked, "How can I help you? I'm a busy man, so make this quick."

"Let's start with you explaining the gifts under the tree," I said.

"Thanks, Dash." Rob placed a hand on my forearm. "I think we know how to question him on our own."

When Everett's face paled, the red of his eyes popped even more. "You want to question me about a few presents for charity?"

"Presents for charity?" Rob and I both spoke at once.

When he shot me a glare, I squished my lips together with two fingers and let him resume questioning.

"Which charity?"

"Some kid thing," Everett said. "The organizer called it Budding Futures or Building Futures. Something like that. They requested the petting zoo to draw more families to the market. Like we needed animals for that at Christmas."

Rob made a couple notes in his book. "Who's the organizer?"

"May Chaney."

"Victor's wife?" I asked. The mishmash of puzzle pieces in my head began to shift into place. When both Rob and Alex appeared confused, I added, "Swordfish guy."

"Yeah." Everett brightened. "Victor was on our Board of Directors for ten years. He got arrested earlier this year on some lame drug charge. May's been trying to raise money to get him a good lawyer but not having much luck."

That didn't surprise me. From what I knew, Victor was about as popular as Covid, which was why I was the only PI gullible enough to take his case. "So, she's distracting herself with a new charity?"

Everett shrugged. "I guess so. Can I go now? I need to keep the vendors from leaving early. This entire day has become a giant headache."

"There's a great crowd and most of them are buying," Alex pointed out. "Why would any of them want to leave early?"

"First, the animals got loose, then the rash of thefts ..."

Rob frowned. "Thefts?"

"Despite the police presence, every booth has lost one or two items. I've compiled a list If you're interested."

I shook my head and muttered, "Why would the police be interested to hear about thefts?"

Alex cleared his throat. Loudly.

My focus returned to the gigantic Christmas tree as Rob and Alex perused the list attached to Everett's clipboard. If a thief was desperate to steal enough items to resell and couldn't escape unnoticed, they might take advantage of the free wrapping booth to hide them in plain sight.

All except the goat, which was where my brilliant spark of an idea fizzled. How could someone giftwrap and hide a goat?

I sat on one of the wooden benches facing the tree.

Did the farmer steal his own goat to have an excuse not to show up at the market anymore? If so, bringing a fainting llama could've been a key part of his plan. Except that Gumdrop seemed to be an even bigger hit than anyone expected.

Everett's body language—the fact his attention was focused elsewhere even as two police officers questioned him—made me suspicious. His feet pointed sideways toward the market rather than forward. He twitched like he'd soaked in a vat of coffee overnight. True, he might've been concerned the whole event was falling apart, but his behavior alone was enough to add him to my suspect list.

That snarky elf also made my short list. No pun intended. What if he was in cahoots with his cousin's wife, May?

Cahoots. I liked that word. I planned to use it more often.

Leaving the cops behind, I wandered through the market, passing half a dozen Santas on my way to the Building Young Futures booth twenty feet north of the petting zoo. Before I'd even approached the table, May Chaney shot me a glare that would've withered me if I wasn't so stubborn and on a mission.

"Hello, thank you for stopping by," she said with a Southern twang. I figured she was only being nice to me because of the family with two young kids nearby. "Have you head of Building Young Futures?"

She wore a nametag with colored lights that flashed against her cheery red blouse. Her hair, once drab and blunt to her shoulders, was in a cute, silver pixie cut. It gave her a professional look.

"Only a couple minutes ago from the organizer." I forced a sickeningly sweet smile and hoped she'd figure out I was onto her scam.

She mimicked my insincerity. Replying in a falsetto voice that grated on my nerves, "We are a not-for-profit group raising money to provide children in need with hot lunches and tutoring."

"Sounds like a noble cause," I replied as the parents ushered the kids toward the petting zoo.

The minute I was alone with May, her sunshiny demeanor vanished, and she whispered, "I know who you are.

"Here we go. It wasn't my fault."

"You're the one who found the llama for Henry."

Not what I expected to hear. "Huh? Yeah."

Up the street, Gumdrop let out another yell before a new crowd of shoppers clapped and cheered. If this kept up, he'd develop an ego. Or brain damage.

"I'm so glad," May gushed. "Gumdrop is such a hoot! People are dropping more money in Santa's gift bag than we expected."

My ears prickled. "Santa's gift bag?"

"Well, we couldn't exactly copy the other holiday charities and use a kettle, could we? We decided to use a big ole velvet gift bag."

"Yeah, that's original." I wondered what else Santa's gift bag held. Darn, I should've taken a look at Everett's list.

Excusing myself, I made a beeline for the petting zoo. Sure enough, there was the same portly Santa in the burgundy suit that I'd seen when I found Gumdrop on the beach, and again near the Christmas tree earlier. His belly full of jelly had shifted again, this time to the left as he held open a two-foot-long burgundy bag for shoppers to drop in their donations.

I dug a dollar out of my pocket and stood next to him. "I had no idea Santa took donations."

He glared, then said gruffly, "Economy's tough all over. It's for the kids."

"Which charity?"

"I dunno. Some scholarship thing."

"Wrong answer." With a frown, I used my dollar to buy a cup of pellets from Henry to feed the animals.

The chickens and pig were starting to settle for naps from being overfed. Before I could get close to any of them, Gumdrop spit in my direction. Then he fainted.

"That routine's getting old, pal," I called out before turning to Henry. "Doesn't he ever get tired of that?"

He shrugged. "It gets hard on him after a while, but he refuses to go back into the trailer. He loves the kids."

"Yeah, well he hates me."

"Because he spits at you? Don't take it personal. He's a drama llama. If he was human, he'd be on Broadway."

"You mean it's all an act?"

Henry grinned. "If he didn't like you, he'd ignore you."

"Hilarious." I watched Santa stuff a twenty in his right pocket, then slip a man something from his left. "Hey, Henry? How did you find out about this Building Young Futures group?"

"Who?" His eyebrows squished together.

I motioned toward Santa. "The group collecting money for the charity. The people who invited you."

"Never heard of 'em," he said. "I got a call from Everett weeks ago saying he wanted me here for the Christmas market. He must've forgot, cause when I got here, he had no idea. They had to make room for the pens. Then some yahoo fell into a fence panel and Gumdrop and a few others got out. You know the rest."

"But you're still missing the Angora goat."

Henry nodded. "Yup. An expensive Angora goat. I got the cops and my wrangler, Keith, lookin' for her. I need to keep an eye on the rest of 'em."

"Is Keith trustworthy?"

"Been with me ten years. He's the one who usually does this public crap, but with Gumdrop here, we needed the two of us."

I chuckled. "I take it Gumdrop's your problem child."

The llama sat in the straw eyeballing me from behind the fence. Probably looking for the nearest exit to come after me.

"Nah. He hates Keith, is all. Won't do a thing he says."

Another piece of the puzzle floated around in my head. "Where's Keith now?"

"Like I said, he went off lookin' for Daisy when the fence fell. I ain't seen him since."

"I take it Daisy's the goat." I should've just asked its name to begin with. It would've saved so much of my sanity. "Did Keith ride with you or did he bring his own truck?"

Henry smirked. "If you're thinkin' he stole her, you're flat out wrong. He's afraid of Daisy, too."

"Yet he's an animal wrangler who went to look for her and hasn't come back."

"He's more afraid of Gumdrop than he is of Daisy."

Some animal wrangler. I pinched the bridge of my nose. "He does know how much Daisy's worth though, right?"

"That he does."

"Mwah," Gumdrop said again. This time he nodded toward the beach.

Call me crazy, but I glanced back over my shoulder, then told him, "Yeah, I like the beach, too. I'll bet you enjoyed rolling in the sand, didn't you?"

"You didn't happen to see Daisy when you ran into Gumdrop, did you?" Henry asked. "Both of 'em headed that way when they run off."

"Not really." When Gumdrop bleated again and nodded toward the beach, I got an idea. An awful idea that he was trying to communicate—or make a break for it. Geez, from P.I. to llama whisperer in a mere couple of hours. "Look, this is gonna sound weird, but can I borrow Gumdrop for a few minutes?"

He seemed hesitant at first, then shrugged. "He's taken a shine to you so... Sure. Long as I get him back soon. Market ends at three."

I handed him my business card. "It's not like I have much use for a fainting llama. I'll have him back in less than an hour, or you can send the police after me. Trust me, they all know where to find me."

When Henry opened the pen, Gumdrop sat perfectly still as though he knew what was going on. Henry clipped a leash somewhere deep inside the mass of fur on her neck before leading Gumdrop out of the pen.

He handed me the other end and asked, "Should I get one of the cops to go with you?"

"I'm bonded," I assured him.

"Yeah, but you're a mite of a thing. You sure you're strong enough to control him?"

"I got this." My false bravado kicked in just as Gumdrop spit at me.

The gob landed in the exact same spot as it had on the beach. Right in the middle of my chest. He was definitely a sharpshooter. If he kept it up, I'd offer him to the military.

I led the drama llama around the market rather than straight through where flowers and chocolates would tempt us both to nibble. By the time we neared the beach, a parade of children followed begging me to let them ride him. Their parents were willing to pay big money for the photo op.

Burgundy Santa followed, kindly offering to help gather the funds.

I snorted. "Yeah, I'll bet."

By the time we reached the sand, Gumdrop snorted, fed up with all of us. He reared up, then took off at a run dragging me in the sand behind him. We beelined across the beach toward the playground near the skateboard park.

I closed my eyes and mouth to keep out the sand he kicked into the air behind him and ran cartoon-like in bare feet. My flip-flops fell off along the way, but I managed to hang onto my precious Christmas packages. Just not my dignity. I lost that with my shoes.

The entire time, the llama screamed like an ambulance siren, "Mwah! Mwah!"

It was as if he was calling someone. Or something. Cries echoed back to us. Along with a voice begging for help.

As Gumdrop slowed his pace to a trot, I regained my footing in the sand. Peering over his furry back at the playground fifty feet off the beach, I spied a man on the playground platform. A gray, long-haired goat paced below. Now and then, the goat made a run at the lower part of the yellow plastic slide.

"It's about time!" the man shrieked. "That thing's nuts."

Gumdrop sauntered over to nuzzle Daisy's head. While he calmed the goat, I looked up at the man on the playground platform. About five foot nine, wearing a plaid shirt and jeans with a red nose on a string hanging around his neck, he had to be Henry's missing wrangler as well as the clown I'd seen on the beach earlier.

"Are you Keith?" I asked.

The herd of kids, parents, and the gasping Santa were closing the gap. We didn't have long.

"Yeah." He pointed toward the animals. "That goat's crazy. I've been trying to get away from it for hours."

I nodded toward Daisy and Gumdrop who cuddled in the warm sand together. "So's the llama. He looks fine now though. I guess he missed his friend."

When Keith headed for the ladder, Gumdrop gave a weird hiss like he was deflating. Keith flinched and backed away before sitting near the top of the slide, not relaxed, yet no longer flat out terrified. I texted Rob our location and told him to bring backup and a handful of llama treats.

"Did you catch Daisy when she escaped, or were you trying to steal her?" I asked.

No time to waste. Santa and the mob was less than fifty yards away. My heart sank. There was no way the police would show up before things went totally sideways.

Keith clutched his head in his hands. "I was supposed to hide Daisy until Henry offered a reward, then my partner would turn her in to the authorities. Since that goat's worth a lot of money, we figured we'd get a few grand easy."

"That's why you let all the animals loose, isn't it?"

"It seemed like a good idea at the time." Keith looked around the playground. "Until I got stuck up here."

Santa snarled. "What are you doing up there? You were supposed to load that thing in my truck and clear out of town."

"About that ..." Keith gestured toward the animals.

Santa fished inside his suit. Just as the rest of the crowd caught up to us, he waved a gun in my direction. "You. Get those people outta here."

I held my hands up at my sides. "Oh, man! I hate people more than animals."

"Move it, Dash," he ordered.

My eyes widened. "How do you...?"

Santa turned to Keith before I could get a better look and snarled, "Get those two in the truck. Now."

Fresh beads of sweat broke out on the wrangler's face. "You don't understand. Those two are evil."

Santa reached over and grabbed the goat by the collar. "It's not difficult. Get down here, grab hold of this thing..."

Gumdrop's spit coated the side of Santa's face causing him to reel back and release Daisy's collar in surprise.

While a couple kids cried when the llama attacked Santa, most cheered Gumdrop on.

"This is not going to end well," I muttered, and managed to move a couple feet closer before Santa turned the gun on me again. With crying kids and angry parents in harm's way, I did the only thing I could think of. I pointed and yelled, "You're not the real Santa."

His eyes grew wide. "What are you doing?"

Keith took advantage of the diversion to hit the ground running. He was well past the mob before his partner noticed. That was when Santa swung the gun around and swore. Everyone behind him dove onto the sand.

"See," I told the kids. "The real Santa wouldn't have a gun or swear."

"He just might in his line of work," Santa said. "Toys cost a fortune these days."

"You might as well give up," I took another tentative step closer. "You have too many witnesses. There's no way you're getting out of here with that goat. Not if the llama has anything to say about it."

Santa grabbed hold of Daisy's collar once more. "Watch me."

I did.

I watched as Gumdrop scrambled to his feet, headbutted the big man in red, and sent him flying up the slide. The kids cheered as fake Santa slid back down before the llama pushed him right back up like a yoyo.

Before Gumdrop could ram him a third time, Henry, Rob, and Alex raced in front of him to intervene. They placed handcuffs on the nasty Santa before Alex tugged off his synthetic beard.

"Victor?" How had I not recognized him? Okay, aside from the shifting padding, the fake facial hair, and the beady eyes.

"You're under arrest again, Chaney," Rob announced. "See what happens if you're not good, kids? You go to jail."

I tapped his shoulder and pointed to the wrangler still running across the beach. "That's his accomplice, but you might want to go easy on him. Technically, the only thing he did was to let the animals loose then get cornered by the goat."

"I'll keep that in mind," Rob said. "Just stay out of the way."

"Happily." I began to walk away.

Alex called after me, "Where are you going? We need your statement."

"To Ricardo's for a cold drink. I was just dragged across the beach by a llama who's in love with a goat. I might need therapy after this."

Ignoring their shouts, I continued toward the sidewalk hoping to find my flip-flops—and maybe a lost shaker of salt, as Jimmy Buffett would say. Thankfully, my flip-flops were still intact. Somehow, I'd lost them ten feet apart from each other.

Chuckling, I stuck in my earbuds and searched for another Jimmy Buffett Christmas song as I carried my flip-flops toward Ricardo's with visions of frozen lemonade dancing in my head. *Mele Kalikamaka* filled my ears and soothed my soul.

Along with a loud, "Mwah."

I shrieked and turned around, ending up nose to nose to nose with Gumdrop and Daisy, who was bigger than I'd realized.

Back at the playground, Rob held his phone to his ear. Santa sat on the end of the slide with one kid after another climbing onto his lap. Alex leaned against the playground laughing so hard his face was red and shiny with tears.

Focusing on my furry companions, I shrugged. "You guys look like you could use a drink. Come on. First round's on me."

When we passed the flamingoes, Daisy nipped off one of their hats. All I could do was shrug and call out, "Hey, Ricardo, three frozen lemonades for me and my friends, *por favor*."

He peered out the window with a grin. Then he closed his eyes, shook his head, and took a second look. "Is this the llama?"

I nodded. "Ricardo, meet Gumdrop and his friend, Daisy."

"You were not joking."

Placing a ten-dollar bill on the counter, I asked him to put their drinks in bowls.

"Keep the money, Dash," he said. "All I want are pictures for social media."

By the time Rob, Alex, and Henry came to retrieve the animals, we were two drinks and several photos in. Plus, I'd told them half my life story. Gumdrop hadn't spit at me once. He even let me sit between he and Daisy for a while.

"Come on, guys." Henry grasped their leads and clicked his tongue. "Time to go home. Sorry they've been so much trouble, Miss."

"Call me Dash." I handed him my business card, then and patted them both. "No trouble. They're kind of fun when they're hanging out together. I had no idea they like frozen lemonade. I guess they're not all bad."

Gumdrop stuck out his lower lip, yelled "Mwah," then spit at me one last time. Direct hit to the chest.

"Hey. I thought we were friends," I shouted.

Both Gumdrop and Daisy fell over into the sand. When I gasped, they gazed up and, I swear to the stars, they both winked and grinned.

With the market packed up, the bad guys in a cage, and the petting zoo gone, the only thing left was to hand over the Christmas gifts I'd bought. I hoped nothing broke during the commotion. Elegantly wrapped in the brown paper bags from the vendor, I presented them with their gifts.

"This is the best seasoning going," Alex gushed. "How'd you know?"

"Good guess," I admitted.

Rob sniffed the oil things I'd picked out. "Sandalwood."

"And the weight bench cleaner has some antibacterial something or another," I pointed out. I hadn't listened close enough to remember what.

Alex pulled a card out of his pocket. "Thanks, Dash. I have something for you, too."

I tugged out the Christmas card and discovered a laminated card inside. "A get out of jail free card? Is this from a Monopoly board game?"

"I thought it might come in handy. The chief signed the back, so it's all official. Minor offenses only."

Laughing, I hugged him. "I'll keep it in my pocket. Just in case. Thanks."

"Merry Christmas, Dash. See you two around." He strolled toward the parking lot, checking his phone. Probably for the photos he'd snapped of me and my furry friends to show his wife and kids.

Rob grinned. "You know those pictures will come back to haunt you."

"As long as Gumdrop and Daisy don't. I've had my fill of critters for a while."

He held out a hand. "Let's walk."

"What? I thought we were doing Christmas gifts."

"Yours is up the beach."

Folding my arms across my chest, I warned him, "If it's a llama, you're going to have a lonely New Year."

"No llama. And, before you ask, no goat either."

"Okay." I took his hand, and we walked up the beach past the playground to the skatepark. At the top of the hill, he sat on the grass and motioned for me to sit next to him.

"A picnic?" I asked. "I don't see any food. Oh, and if you get up on one knee, I'm heading for home."

He patted the grass beside him again. "It's only been a few months, but I wanted to give you something special and this is the perfect spot."

"Where we had a picnic while looking for skateboard thieves before you threw your back out?" I asked. "I suppose that's kind of romantic."

Rob handed me a small box. "Merry Christmas, Dash."

My heart in my throat, I opened it to reveal a gold chain with a glittering, elongated pendant. "Is that ...?"

"A skateboard. The design is a hand painted witch. A souvenir to remember our last case together."

I burst out laughing, then hugged him. "It's perfect!"

"Good," he said. "My backup gift was a stuffed llama, but I was pretty sure you'd hit me with it."

"Mwah." I laughed until tears streamed from my eyes.

- The End -

THE CAT LADY'S SECRET

DIANE BATOR

DASH ALLMAN MYSTERIES BOOK 5

The Cat Lady's Secret

Dash Allman PI, Book 5

Diane Bator

Escape With a Writer Publishing

A soft purr made me stir slightly from a weird dream. When the sound continued, I rolled onto my back with a sigh and muttered, "Ten more minutes, Mom."

The sound persisted.

Then a weight settled on my chest, and something tickled my chin. Reaching to push it away, I ended up with a handful of fur.

"Oh, no! Not that llama again!" I rolled over so fast that a small, furry body flew to my left. Since I didn't own a cat—nor did I even like cats—the sight of a pure black one wearing a green collar on my bed made me scoot back toward my pillows.

"How did you get in here? This place is critter proof." I'd made sure of that after meeting Gumdrop, the Drama Llama, and his friend, Daisy the goat.

The cat gave a soft meow and pawed at something rectangular on the bed. Wary, I inched closer. It was a tarot card. Not one of those fancy oracle cards with dragons, unicorns, or butterflies, but the old school kind with royalty, cups, and wands.

This one was Death, who looked about as happy to see me as I was to see him.

"Where did you get that?" I asked, before realizing the cat couldn't tell me. If it did, I wouldn't have bothered going out the door. I would've aimed for the nearest window and into the ocean where it couldn't follow.

The cat stepped over the card and sauntered closer as though expecting me to touch it.

"Back off, kitty. I like cats even less than llamas."

Holding up my fingers up in front of it, I made the sign of a cross. Not that I was religious. Nor was the cat a vampire. It was just one of those reflex things. The cat sniffed my fingers, then licked them. Light reflected off the tiny key on its collar.

I looked around for an open window or door. Nothing. The cat was scrawny as though it hadn't eaten in a while. Even so, there was no way it could've crawled through the mail slot.

Feeling the call of nature, I told the cat not to move and went into the bathroom. Instantly, I felt a draft and swore. The window between the small vanity and the toilet was broken. Bits of black fur stuck to the jagged glass. How did such a small cat manage to break the window?

The bottom edge of the broken glass was dotted with more blood. From as calm as the cat was on my bed, I doubted the blood belonged to it. Its desire to get inside wouldn't have been so strong as to try to slice open its belly. Not with the weather so balmy.

I guessed my furry guest had help.

Returning to my bedroom, my gaze landed on the tarot card. Somehow, I couldn't picture the cat selecting the Death card and bringing it over to my house for the fun of it.

Someone was sending me a message.

The only person I could think of was the gray-haired cat lady next door. The black cat had to be one of her animals. It was skinny and a bit roughed up. I would've fed it if I had anything but two cans of beer in the fridge.

Did cats like stale crackers? Those I might have.

Leaving the tarot card on the bed, I hoisted the cat into the air. It wore a shiny green collar with a small, gold key attached, which seemed like an odd thing to put on a cat's collar. "Okay, buddy. Me and you are going next door. I'll bet that's where you came from, isn't it?"

The cat gave a soft mew and reached its paws toward the bed. It didn't seem to have the same desire to get to the bottom of things as I did.

Leaving the yawning critter amid the crumpled blankets, I rummaged for a pair of flip-flops near the front door, then strolled out into the sunshine.

I paused at my gate, as always, to check both ways for errant witches on skateboards, llamas, and goats. The list seemed to grow longer with each case. Thankfully, all I saw today was the sparkling blue ocean, miles of sand, and dancing palm trees.

The house next door to mine was nearly identical. Same peeling blue paint. Same sagging eaves that thumped against the warped siding in storms. The biggest difference was my front yard was tidy with flowers that peeked through the white gravel. The cat lady's front yard was overgrown and possibly hid dangerous creatures. Like cats and vacuum cleaner salesmen.

When I knocked on the front door, it swung open. The powerful scents of ammonia, feces, and something metallic met my nostrils. I gasped for a breath and covered my nose before poking my head inside and calling out, "Hello? Anyone here?"

No reply aside from a serious of hisses and meows from beyond a doorway covered with a faded black curtain.

I started to shout again but realized I didn't even know her name. Yelling, "Hey, Cat Lady," would be kind of rude.

Despite the smell only a cat lady could love, I took a few tentative steps inside. The front room was the same size as mine—about ten feet by ten feet—only much neater. She had walnut cabinets stocked with tarot cards, books, crystals, and evil eye decorations.

No sign of cats anywhere in the front room, aside from the smell.

Sheer red curtains covered the large front window giving the room a creepy glow. Dark purple velvet draped over a three-foot round table to my right. Two plain wooden chairs sat opposite a large, high-backed one covered with more purple velvet. Odd. The few times I'd seen the cat lady, she certainly hadn't come off so flamboyant.

More frump than fortune teller.

Growls and meows came from beyond the doorway. I reached for the thin, black bedsheet over the door and moved it to one side. In an instant, the house went from Fortune Teller Chic to Hoarder Heaven. Boxes, bins, plastic bags, assorted cats, clothes, and broken bits of unidentifiable items were stacked from floor to cracked plaster ceiling. I guessed the cat lady hadn't parted with anything she loved for twenty or thirty years.

She could've had any number of secrets hidden in that little beach front cottage. For that matter, she could've had an entire football team in her living quarters, and I wouldn't have been able to see them for the cats, boxes, piles of clothing, and stacks of newspapers and magazines. Everywhere there wasn't a cat, there was evidence of cats.

I shuddered, covering my nose just as something licked my foot. At least five cats swarmed my bare feet. The guardians of the back room either assumed I was trespassing, or lunch.

Quickly scanning the few cats, I could see I counted ten more and winced. Was this where the kitty who'd made itself a nest on my bed had lived until now?

Backing away, I decided to focus on the front room to see what I could learn. A business card laying face up on the velvet-covered table proclaimed her to be Madame Twyla. A professional psychic for fifty years. "One hundred percent accurate."

How could I have lived next door to a cat-crazed fortune teller all these years without knowing? Some private detective I was.

Near the table was a puddle of something dark. As I tugged my flip-flop out of the sticky goo, I realized it was blood. I looked around in case I missed seeing a body.

Nothing in the chair or on the floor. There were marks on the carpet that led to the kitchen. Had the cats...?

I barely finished that thought as a large, orange tabby prowled toward me. I took a step back. "Nice, kitty. Down, kitty. I'm just looking for your boss. Please don't hurt me."

It sat in front of the black sheet draped across the doorway that led to the mess beyond.

"Don't worry. I won't go back there without a sherpa and a bag of kibble." I pulled out my phone to do a search. Did Jimmy Buffett have a song to soothe cats? I know he had one about his dog. Maybe something soft and calming about pirates or the Southern Cross.

The front door opened behind me. When I spun around, two uniformed police officers burst inside with their guns drawn and trained on me. Instinctively, I raised my hands high in the air.

Alex Carson was the first to enter the cat lady's cottage. He'd wisely worn short sleeves in the surging heat of the day. "What are you doing here?"

I lowered my hands in relief and bent over to wipe my flip-flop on the carpet as I said, "Probably the same thing you are."

"We're investigating a break and enter," the other cop announced.

"You're under arrest." I judged him as not so smart considering the long shirt sleeves in the heat. Rookie mistake. He'd regret that by noon.

Alex holstered his weapon. "Cool it, Rambo. This is Dash Allman. She lives next door. Dash, this is Vic Ralston."

"Dash?" Ralson asked with a grin. "Did your mother hate you?"

The joke in my family was that my mom hated me, but loved Dashiell Hammett, which really sucked for the little girl she named Dashiell Allman. Not funny.

I glanced from the cop with the moustache back to Alex and decided to let the rookie off the hook. For now. "Where's your usual partner?"

Officer Rob Gwynn was my off-and-on boyfriend, whom I hadn't heard from in a few weeks. I guessed he was either dead or I'd done something to tick him off again. Last time, I drugged him. In my defense, he was in pain from wrenching his back.

"Rob had back surgery. He'll be off for a while."

As I walked toward the officers, Ralston took a step back. I ignored him and said, "Oh wow. No wonder he hasn't called. I guess those skateboard tricks really put him out of commission. No more undercover work for him for a while."

"Nope." Alex gazed around the room, then flinched and motioned for me and Ralston to return outside with him.

I glanced toward the black sheet over the doorway where five cats now guarded the rest of the house. Holding my hands up at my sides, I backed away slowly.

Once outside, Ralston closed the front door. "Shouldn't we secure the scene?"

"I wouldn't go any farther without a respirator," I told him. "From what I saw, there are a lot of cats in the rest of the house."

Alex snapped at him to put away his gun before he hurt himself. Then he sent Ralston to call the Animal Shelter to get rid of the cats before they made a bigger mess of the crime scene.

Ralston finally put away the gun, then asked, "What were you doing in Freida Wassenberg's house?"

"Is that what her name is?" I asked. "I just knew her as the cat lady. She had a card on the table that said—"

"Why were you inside?" he repeated.

I sat on the wooden bench in the shade of her porch, careful to avoid the broken slat. "I woke up with a black cat on my bed. Somehow, it got in through a broken window in my bathroom and brought me a tarot card."

He scoffed. "A likely story."

"You don't know Dash," Alex said, then turned to face me. "Which card?"

"Death."

Ralston frowned. "And now there's blood on the floor. Coincidence?"

I raised my eyebrows. "I'd say so since cats can't read."

"I'm going to call the Animal Shelter." His face reddened.

Once Ralston was out of earshot, I met Alex's gaze. "What did you do to get stuck with that clown?"

Alex chuckled. "He's not so bad."

"I've met smarter hammers."

He sat next to me and said, "He's a rookie. They paired him with me hoping he'd learn something. This is our first call together."

"And now you're stuck with me too, because I was at the crime scene."

After a long moment, I asked, "You're not even going to ask about my broken window, are you?"

Alex shrugged. "I figured you'd bring it up if it was important."

"Considering it wasn't broken when I went to bed last night, I think it might be. It looks like that was how the cat got in."

"You didn't hear the glass break?" He frowned.

"I've had nightmares since the whole llama thing. I took one of those sleeping pills I fed Rob. If something did happen at the cat lady's house last night, I didn't hear it."

"I'm going to pretend I didn't hear part of that."

"The part about Rob?" I asked.

He tapped his index finger on the end of his nose.

"Hey, Alex?" His temporary partner returned up the sidewalk. "They wanna know how many cats are inside."

Alex looked to me for an answer.

"I'd say at least fifty."

"Fifty?" Ralston's eyes grew wide.

I waved my hand toward the door. "You wanna go inside and count?"

"I'm good." When he repeated my estimates into the phone, I could hear someone ask if he was serious. He ended the call and reported back to Alex that someone would arrive in twenty minutes.

Alex gave a nod. "Good job, Ralston. You guard the door. I'm going next door to check out Dash's broken window."

"Wait. You're Dash Allman the detective?" he asked.

Alex and I exchanged glances before I nodded, sure I could see an itty bitty light bulb flickering over Ralston's head.

Wary, I replied, "Yeah. Why?"

"Rob warned me I might run into you," he said. "I'm supposed to believe whatever you say, because you have good instincts. Right now, I'm starting to think he's full of crap."

Clearing his throat, Alex took me by the upper arm. "I'm going next door to see if Dash's broken window has anything to do with the blood next door. Stay here and don't let anyone inside until forensics and the Animal Shelter arrive."

"I didn't call forensics," Ralston replied.

"Did you see any blood on the floor?" Alex asked.

"I'll call forensics."

Alex paraded me down the sidewalk to my cottage next door and into my backyard. I didn't have to point out the bathroom window since it was the only one that had broken glass with fur stuck to it.

"Where's the cat now?" he asked.

I shrugged. "Witness protection. I left it on my bed when I went over to the cat lady's house to ask her about it. I have no idea where it went from there."

Since my bathroom window was on the ground floor and barely big enough for me to squeeze through, there was no way a big guy like Alex Carson could get in. He looked around my overgrown yard where he found a rusty old chair to stand on.

"Don't you believe in keeping your yard tidy?" he asked, peering into the window.

"It's a rental. Besides, it's not like I use it or anything."

Alex sighed. "All the better for people to hide murder weapons at your place."

"What are you talking about?"

He got off the chair, then hid it behind a bushy plant. "Let's go inside, then I'll tell you. Better yet, I'll show you. Then you can rethink your choice of clientele."

We walked around the cottage, then I unlocked the door. Alex beelined toward the bathroom while pulling on a pair of rubber gloves. When he reached the little garbage can beneath the window, he took out his phone and snapped a few photos.

Since I couldn't get around him to see what was inside, I had to wait patiently near the door. That lasted exactly ten seconds before I asked, "What did you find?"

"Something the normally observant Dash Allman missed."

Alex stepped aside for me to take a look. In the bottom of my wastebasket, cushioned by tissues, tampon wrappers, and two empty toilet paper tubes, lay a handgun.

My face burned. "To be fair, the cat woke me up from a deep sleep and I—"

"I'll send the forensic guys over here," He took a few more pictures.

"Great. Now everyone will get to see my trash."

Alex rolled his eyes. "Nothing most of us haven't seen before. I have a wife and two daughters."

That was true.

"You're not going to check it out?" I asked.

"There's glass from the window in the bottom. I don't want to get cut," he told me. "Forensics will just take the whole thing into evidence."

My eyes grew wide. "What? That means I'll have to buy a new trashcan."

"If I were you, I'd get one with a lid," he suggested. "Just in case this happens again."

I snorted and asked, "What are the odds of that?"

"Considering it's you, much higher than the average person." He walked me toward the front door.

As we passed my bedroom, I noticed the black cat was curled on my pillow. I picked it up. "This is the cat who came in through the window with the tarot card. Look, buddy, you can't stay here. Let's go. You and your friends are getting a trip to a nice kitty hotel."

"A kitty hotel?" he asked as he raised his eyebrows. "More like shared accommodations while they get checked out and hope to be adopted."

Something about his tone—or my lack of food—made my stomach lurch. I frowned. "What do you mean?"

He paused with one hand on the doorknob. "If they're sick or the shelter can't find homes for them, some of them might be put down."

I gazed down at the furry bundle cradled on my arm. "Put down? As in—?"

"Euthanized."

My first instinct was to drop the cat on the floor and tell it to run. I couldn't keep it. My landlord would freak out. Besides, I couldn't even keep a houseplant alive. The cat was taking its nine lives into its paws just being in the same room as me.

"Do you think Rob would like a Get Well Cat?" I asked.

The cat pressed closer to me and purred.

I let out a loud groan. "What if I put it on the floor and pretended I never saw it?"

"You're too late," Alex said. "It's adopted you."

Setting the feline in the doorway, I shouted, "Go home. Go."

Both Alex and the cat stared at me as if I was crazy. Alex shook his head before he walked outside. The cat yawned before returning to bed. My bed.

As I closed the front door, I had a funny feeling Alex was right. He...she...whatever it was had unofficially moved in. At least it wasn't a llama or a goat.

The Animal Shelter van parked in front of the cat lady's house. Two men in gray overalls exited the cab of the vehicle and strode toward us. Their bravado reminded me of the Ghostbusters. For a heartbeat, I was afraid of what they'd use to round up the cats.

"Hey, Al whatdasitch?" " one of the men asked, pushing back a threadbare, dark blue, baseball cap.

When the man spat tobacco juice on the lawn, I gagged. Avoiding looking at him, I leaned toward Alex and whispered, "What did he say?"

"He asked what the situation was," Alex told me, then nodded to the older man.

"The victim has a bunch of cats inside," Ralson announced. "We need to access the crime scene without them disturbing anything."

My gut said he was a few hours too late for that.

Alex put Ralston in charge of the crowd that began to gather. "And, for the record, we don't have a victim. Just a pool of blood in the front room."

Tobacco Guy's brown eyes widened. The patch on his overalls read "Hutch". "Where did it go?"

"Should we be on the lookout for zombies?" his associate asked.

I met his gaze with a scowl. He winked and gave me the once over. That's when I realized I was still in my pajamas. Shorts and a thin tank top. No underwear. I cringed and tried to hide behind Alex as he gave them instructions. Tapping his back, I muttered that I was going to get dressed. Preferably into a suit of armor.

"Just don't touch anything," he advised, "especially the gun."

When Wink Guy, whose overalls proclaimed him as "Bobby", followed his partner to the van, I ran back to my house and locked the door. I did not want an audience—especially those two guys. Cuing up a cheery Jimmy Buffett song on my phone to calm me down, I was ready for anything. Except the sight of the cat curled in a ball near my pillow. I turned the volume down. I doubted the cat wanted to dream about sons of sailors.

Since I hadn't seen a collar or tag, I had no idea what to call it. Maybe I'd check in with Rob to see how he was doing and ask if he knew any good names for a black cat.

I inched open the door to my closet and peered inside. Considering how my day had started, I had no idea what to expect. Grateful for no further surprises, I pulled on a padded bra and my frumpiest around-the-house dress. The last thing I wanted was that cat-trapping creep hitting on me again.

By the time I slipped on flip-flops and opened the door, the mob outside had grown from ten to about fifty people. And a news truck. I reached into my house for sunglasses and a floppy hat.

Whoever said there's no such thing as bad press hadn't followed me around for a day. The case I'd helped crack before Christmas with the llama and goat had resulted in several weirdos calling and dropping by to see me. None of them looking for a private detective. They just wanted to see the chick who was dragged down the beach by a llama.

I locked my door, despite the police presence, and searched the crowd for Alex. He was near the cat lady's front door. When he noticed me, he raised his eyebrows and said, "I'm surprised you came back out."

"Why's that?"

"Seriously? After that video footage of you and the llama being chased by Santa down the beach I thought you'd hide from the news crews." When I growled, he chuckled and asked, "How well did you know your neighbor?"

"Obviously, I didn't. I had no idea how many cats were in there, or that she was a fortune teller. Did they find anything?"

Alex shook his head. "Fifty or sixty cats. No bodies other than feline ones. Nobody hiding anywhere in the house."

"Did you send your sidekick inside to clear the house?"

"Not a chance. I left him with crowd control. I can deal with cats better than with gawkers."

I wrinkled my nose. Neither appealed to me. "I'll bet that smelled lovely."

"Don't look so sad," he said. "You'll get your chance to find out soon."

"Wait. What?"

We stepped aside as the two men in overalls each carried out two small cages. Wink Guy flashed me a smile complete with another once over. I cringed as they walked to the back of their van, then returned a couple minutes later with the same cages.

"Where are they putting them all?"

"They have two large crates in the back of the van," Alex said. "With this many animals, they don't have enough carriers for each cat."

After a few more trips to the van, Hutch declared the house cat free. I had my doubts, but Alex motioned for me to follow him inside. We paused long enough to put fabric booties on over our footwear before Alex opened a small jar and held it out.

"What is it?" I asked, wincing at the scent.

"Vicks. The menthol will mask the...other odors."

I copied him in dabbing some below each nostril. As we each pulled on a pair of gloves, my gaze dropped to the blood-soaked carpet. "What happened to... Whoever left that?"

Alex shrugged. "No idea. I didn't find anything unusual."

"Besides fifty or sixty cats, anyway," I muttered. "That's not weird at all."

Taking a deep, mentholated breath, I followed him to the doorway. The black sheet lay draped over a chair nearby. The room beyond hadn't changed aside from the lack of felines. The acrid smell made me gasp and take a step back. Hadn't the cat lady ever heard of cleaning litter boxes?

"Be careful where you step," Alex answered my silent question.

I began to wish I'd worn hip waders instead of flip-flops with booties over top. My stomach—thankfully still empty—grew queasy.

As we poked around on the narrow paths allotted us by the clutter, which made me a bit claustrophobic. I tried to breathe through my mouth when I could, but my eyes watered from the overpowering scents of ammonia and death. Alex was right. Not all the cats had made it to the van. My heart broke as I thought about the black cat curled on my bed and the cruel fate it had escaped.

"I think I'll call him Lucky," I blurted out.

Alex stopped so suddenly, I ran into his back. He glanced over his shoulder with a scowl. "I hope you're talking about the cat and not Bobby. I saw how he looked at you."

"Who's Bobby?"

He chuckled. "Never mind. Lucky, the black cat. Sounds appropriate for you."

Continuing through the house, we didn't find any human bodies – living or dead. Nor anyone hiding in fear.

Alex led me into the backyard and radioed the forensics team that it was their scene. They'd have their hands full with the mess inside. I felt bad for whoever had to take it all out and sort it.

The sunshine temporarily blinded me, but I was sure I saw something move behind the bushes at the far end of the yard. I pointed and told Alex, "Over there."

We both raced toward the corner, dodging rusty bicycles, saggy mattresses, and car parts. I lost a bootie and a flip-flop while hopping over an overstuffed garbage bag. Pausing to retrieve it, I caught sight of someone in my yard.

"There's a hole in the fence," I shouted to Alex.

He darted behind the bushes.

Rather than keep running, I made a split-second decision to jump over the six-foot high fence despite the wobble. Halfway over, I remembered I was wearing a dress and one flip-flop. The hem caught on a nail at the top and tore.

Too much adrenaline surged through me to stop now. I leaped off the fence onto a figure in a black hoodie and black pants. We both rolled across the grass and came to a stop near a small fruit tree I had no idea was there.

"Freeze!" Alex shouted, wheezing as he strode toward us with his gun drawn.

Rather than freeze, I climbed onto the intruder's back to pin them down.

"Get off me!" a woman yelled. "I'm old. You'll break my bones."

Alex and I exchanged surprised glances. I hopped to my feet to give her space to roll over. The cat lady sneered at me as she sat up.

"Who wants to know?" she snapped.

I gazed at his uniform and weapon and wondered if she was blind. "Freida?"

Alex holstered his gun. "Alex Carson. I did a wellness check on you last week."

"Oh, that's right," she said. "You brought me lunch."

"You did?" I asked. "You didn't bring me anything."

"Drop it, Dash."

Freida ran a hand to tidy her red hair as she turned to me. "Dash? Oh. You're the crazy llama lady I heard about. I've seen you chasing men on the beach."

"Fugitives," I explained when Alex smirked. "Bad guys."

"I know what fugitives are. You don't have to explain your love life to me," he teased, helping Freida to her feet. "As for you, what's with the blood in your house?"

She bowed her head then peeled off her hoodie. The colorful blouse beneath was soaked with blood. "I got him good."

"Who?" we asked in unison.

"The creep who broke in to take my prized possession."

"Which prized possession is that?" Alex asked.

"My cat," Frieda said.

Considering the Animal Shelter had removed more than fifty cats, I frowned. "Was one a pure bred or something?"

She groaned and flicked my forehead. Her hand smelled like something that made me cringe. "Not those cats. The statue that sat on my table where I did my readings. You know the one."

I shook my head and reminded her, "I've never been inside your house until today. How would I know?"

Her thin eyebrows rose. She seemed surprised to hear that, which struck me as odd. Was she senile, or...?

"Can you describe it?" Alex asked, pulling out his notebook. "A photo of it would be even better."

As he questioned her, I noticed a draft on my backside. Sure enough, I'd torn a hole in my dress dangerously close to the bottom of my underwear. One the size of a dinner plate. The only access to the front door of my house was in plain sight of the television cameras.

"I need to go change before my underwear makes the six o'clock news," I told Alex. "Can you shield me from the cameras?"

Freida took off her black hoodie. The blue shirt beneath it had a large, purple stain that appeared fresh. "Here, honey. Take this."

Alex and I exchanged glances before I thanked her. I wrapped it around my waist and darted into my house leaving Alex to deal with the cat lady and her blood-stained shirt. When I took off the hoodie and dropped it on the bedroom floor, Lucky leaped off the bed and took a keen interest in it. He sniffed the dark fabric before he licked it.

I picked up the hoodie, then noticed the same scent Lucky had. "Eww! Please tell me that's not what I think it is."

I hung it on the corner of the closet door before peeling off my dress. The entire area the hoodie had covered was spotted with blood that wasn't mine. My hands began to shake. Had the cat lady killed someone in her front room?

Lucky ignored my angst in favor of pawing at the door to reach the black fabric.

Dressing quickly. I pulled on shorts and a t-shirt, then I dropped the hoodie into a plastic bag. Much to the cat's dismay. I opened the front door and came face to face with a member of the forensics team wearing a white, disposable full body suit.

"I hear you have part of the crime scene here," he said. His eyes were the color of ripe limes, and a shallow dimple burrowed into his left cheek as he smiled. For a half second, I thought he'd throw me a compliment or try to flirt. Then he added, "Hey, you're the lady with the llama."

I cursed beneath my breath and nearly threw the plastic bag at his head. Instead, I held it out to him. "Here. You deal with this. I need to talk to Alex."

His face fell in disappointment. "You're leaving? I was hoping to get your autograph. My kids love watching that video of Santa chasing you and the llama on YouTube."

My face burned. What little good humor I had left succumbed to the flames. I stormed over to where Alex, Ralston, and Frieda stood on Frieda's front porch. The cat lady had changed clothes but seemed even more agitated as Ralston spoke. It seemed like they knew each other.

When I motioned to Alex, he joined me near the fence. "What's up?"

"That black hoodie was soaked with blood," I whispered.

"So were her pants and shirt. I called for backup and we're searching the backyard."

A chill went through me as I recalled losing my flip-flop on something that made me slip. "Do you think she killed the real cat lady?"

"What do you mean?" he frowned.

I glanced toward the red-haired woman. "The only woman I've ever seen here had gray hair and tattered clothes. Frieda, or whoever she is, hasn't asked once about her precious babies and assumed I'd been in her house before."

Alex nodded. "I saw the photo inside of her with another woman. She did something, but I have no idea what. We don't have a body or any sign of the statue she claims is missing. Not even an empty spot in the dust."

"Better check the pawn shops. I'll bet she hocked it." I frowned as my gaze drifted back to my house. Did Lucky have more to do with everything than I thought? "The cat in my house has a collar."

Alex looked at me as though I'd finally lost the last of my marbles. "So?"

"Did any of the other cats have collars?"

"I don't think so."

I grinned. "Lucky's collar has a little gold key attached."

We both glanced toward Frieda who silently pleaded with us to rescue her.

"A key for what?" he whispered.

"No clue," I admitted, "but we need to get that key, and search her house to figure out what it opens."

Alex shook his head. "That's not happening until forensics is done."

Forensics. I turned toward my front door where the man with the amazing green eyes was exiting with a couple bags. The one I gave him, plus what I assumed was my wastebasket and trash.

Lucky followed him to the front door, then sat to take in all the strange humans shouting, taking photos, and eagerly awaiting a body bag or someone in handcuffs. I was probably an early favorite for the handcuffs.

"Is that one of your cats?" Alex asked Frieda.

She meandered toward the fence and narrowed her eyes. "Nope. Don't think so."

I took her arm and led her toward my front door. "Maybe you need a closer look."

Her entire body tensed. Before we got any closer, Lucky stood, arched its back, and hissed. Growling, the cat retreated into my house. I'd bet a hot dog it would've slammed the door if it could.

The green-eyed man gave a nod as he returned to my house.

I folded my arms across my chest and huffed as I followed the cat lady back to her house. "It looked like he got everything to me. I'll bet he went back to snoop in my underwear drawer or something."

"Dash...," Alex warned as a scream came from my house. "Looks like you were right."

"Very funny." I led the way back to my front step and nearly burst out laughing.

The forensics guy was kneeling on a chair while the black cat hissed below him. Its back was arched as it released a guttural growl.

"Someone needs to lock that beast up," he shouted. The fabric of his white suit was torn to shreds at his left ankle.

I crouched and crossed my fingers Lucky wouldn't do the same to my flesh. "Here, kitty. Come on, Lucky."

"Lucky?" the guy asked, then laughed nervously.

When Lucky roared, the guy covered his head with one arm.

"Leave him alone," I said softly.

The cat glanced at me, then purred. He trotted toward me as if not actually possessed by a demon.

"What were you doing?" Alex asked.

As the forensics guy got off the chair, he said, "I noticed the key on its collar. When I reached to look at it, the cat tried to eat me."

I cradled Lucky against my chest. "That would make sense. I have no idea when the poor baby ate last."

"You didn't feed him yet?"

"It's not my cat."

Green Eyes darted toward the front door. "I'll see if I can find some cat food."

Alex examined Lucky's green collar from a couple feet away. "Where's the key?"

"On this side. He didn't take it, if that's what you're thinking, but I'll bet he tried."

When Alex reached out, a growl rumbled against my chest. He backed away slowly and said, "Maybe you'd better do the honors."

"Yeah." I carried Lucky to my bed and sat down. "Okay, buddy, I have no idea if this key means anything, but your owner's in trouble. Can I borrow it to see if we can help? I promise to give it back when I'm done."

In the doorway, Alex cleared his throat. "I can't believe you just asked the cat for permission. The key could become police evidence, you know."

As Lucky rubbed its face against my arm. I glanced up at Alex. "I don't even know if Lucky's a boy or a girl."

"No one taught you how to tell the difference?" he asked. "No wonder you're single."

"I didn't take the time to look. I've been busy." I scowled as I set Lucky on the bed. Instantly, the cat sat and sprawled as cats do to clean its—his—not so private parts.

Alex burst out laughing. "There you go. Just what you needed another man in your life."

Once Lucky eased out of his yoga position, I reached for his collar. "Let's see if this little key can help solve a mystery."

I unfastened his collar, then figured out the clasp that held the key in place. Handing the key to Alex, I returned the collar to Lucky, who strolled toward the pillows and curled up.

"I'll find you some food while I'm at it," I told the cat, then paused I my kitchen to rummage for a bowl. I filled it with water, then set it on the floor.

Alex radioed someone to let them know we'd be over in a couple minutes. I was busy trying to remember what I'd seen in the cat lady's house that would take such a small key. A jewelry box or small safe seemed most likely.

I locked the door behind us and followed Alex past the growing mob on the beach. People were turning the whole sordid thing into a party. Music blared and the smell of barbecue from a food truck filled the air. I drooled. My stomach growled.

Alex pulled me past the cat lady, who peppered Ralston with her own questions. Ralston shot me a glare as I passed him. Her first question was when they'd be done, so she could clean up the mess we were making.

Closing the door behind us, we stood to survey the scene. At first glance, there were no locks the key would fit. After making sure the room had been dusted for prints and evidence secured, we put on gloves and began to open drawers and cupboards.

That was when I found the treasure chest.

"Um, Alex? I'm going to need your help."

He joined me next to the three-foot-long terrarium and crouched next to me to watch two snakes the size of my arms flicking their tongues at us and said, "No way. Not me."

Afraid to avert my eyes, I watched them slither over each other as I pointed out, "You don't have to touch them. Just get that little treasure chest out of there."

"I know just the man for the job." Alex abandoned me with the snakes. A minute later, Ralston appeared and kneeled next to me. "Oh, wow. Pythons. Those things are cool!"

"I'm glad you're excited," I told him. "I need you to grab that little treasure chest."

Ralston stared. "Are you nuts? I hate snakes. Those things are probably poisonous."

"What snakes?" someone asked behind us. Seconds later, Green Eyes leaned next to me. His face lit up like a kid the local bakery. "Oh, cool! Those are Blood Pythons. They're temperamental but they're not poisonous."

"I guess that makes you the man for the job," I told him. "Can you take out that chest?"

When Ralston moved aside, Green Eyes opened the lid, reached into the glass cage, and pulled out the chest as one of snakes attempted to coil around his arm.

"What's in there?" he asked, handing me the chest as he closed the cage.

Shrugging, I glanced at Ralston, noticing a dark stain on his right sleeve. Had he brushed up against the cat lady's clothing and not noticed? "Can you get Alex back in here? I think he needs to see this."

"But I—," Ralston started to argue.

"Please." I blew out a breath the second he left.

"That guy's a weasel. The kids don't like him much," Green Eyes said.

"He knows your kids?"

He nodded. "Yeah. The ones I coach at the community center."

I narrowed my eyes and met his gaze. He was even cuter than I'd first thought. Sandy hair, the eyes, and that dimple...

Before I could get more info, like his name, Alex returned. "Josh, I hear you braved the snakes and got the chest. What's inside?"

I gave my head a shake. I'd already forgotten my mission. Darn hormones.

"We were waiting for you." I fumbled with the key, then jammed it into the lock and gave it a twist. When the lid popped open, we all leaned closer.

"Another key?" Alex asked. "That's just mean."

We all gazed at the terrarium. Thankfully, there were no more chests inside.

Josh chuckled. "Weirdest treasure hunt I've ever been on."

"Don't you have a job to do?" Alex asked as he nudged Josh.

"This is part of my job. We might find more evidence."

I nodded. "He's right. Back to looking for a keyhole. Hopefully, without snakes, or spiders, or cats."

"But snakes are so cute." Josh winked.

His wink had the opposite effect the creepy cat rescue guy's did. My face warmed. Turning back to the snakes, I said, "I'm surprised they haven't gotten loose and eaten the cats. Not like that woman would care."

Alex held up a finger. "The cats. There's a cupboard in the kitchen with a lock."

"I saw it. The one with the funky cats painted on it," Josh added.

I stood with both keys in hand. "Lead the way."

The cupboard in question was one I hadn't noticed earlier when Alex and I walked through. I'd been too distracted by the smells and afraid to find a body. When I'd peeked into the room the first time, three cats were sitting on it.

Alex and Josh cleared a path, then stood back so I could insert the key in the lock. The cabinet was about three feet tall with ornate, curled iron cat tails for handles. It was covered with brightly colored, hand painted cats.

I waited for the click of the lock, then backed away. As I opened the door, I hoped the body we sought wasn't inside.

"Will you look at that," Alex said.

There were dozens of watches, necklaces, rings, and earrings. All of which looked expensive to me. Stacks of money stood to one side along with some other papers.

"Oh, wow! The cat lady's a cat burglar," I announced as Alex called for Ralston to bring Frieda inside.

"Looks like we found more evidence after all," Josh said, raising his camera and snapped several pictures.

Alex asked Josh to move aside, so he could take a closer look. "I'll bet we could match the jewelry up to burglaries all around the city."

Inching my hand toward the stack of papers near the cash, I had to disagree. "I'd say around the country. Those look like boarding passes."

Josh frowned as he continued to take pictures. "Who prints boarding passes anymore? Most people have them on their phones."

"Someone like me who's old school, or who wants a souvenir of the places they've been that they can easily hide or burn," Alex said.

As much as I wanted to grab the passes and thumb through them, I moved out of Alex and Josh's way. Why did none of this make sense? The cat lady—aka Frieda—had a lot of stuff, but I wasn't so sure about the money. And who was the guy she insisted stole her prized possession? If something bad had happened to him, she still wasn't talking.

When the front door opened, Ralston entered dragging Frieda who screamed about police brutality. At least it wouldn't be me on the news this time. The second he closed the door, her shouting stopped, and the cat lady flashed a smile. Weird since I'd never seen her smile in all the years I'd lived next door.

"Well, look at you," she said. "I knew you were a detective, but I never thought you'd put it all together. I've been looking for the key to that thing for two weeks."

Two weeks? It seemed I hadn't put it all together. Not yet. "The black cat was a big help."

Her face paled. "What black cat?"

Alex met my gaze and frowned. "The one at Dash's house who climbed in through her broken window. Pure black with a green collar."

"None of those cats had collars," she said, then scowled. "That dirty, rotten, good for nothing piece of—"

"Your partner?" Alex asked.

"Worse. My sister."

Josh called in his co-worker who'd been in the backyard. Together, they began to catalogue the pieces of jewelry, the money, and the boarding passes. As he spread two of the passes on a clean cloth he spread on a plastic tote, I read the names and gasped. Nudging Alex's arm, I pointed to the passports inside the safe.

When Josh opened them, there were two different, yet similar looking women. Frieda and the other woman could've been twins except for the color of their hair. Their photos made them look more like hardened criminals than tourists.

"There were two cat ladies?" I asked.

"Everything you find will have my prints or my name. That witch took the rest," Frieda told us as she tried to step in front of Alex.

"How?" I asked. "The key to the treasure chest was with Lucky."

Frieda narrowed her eyes. "Who's Lucky?"

"The black cat with the green collar."

She pursed her lips, then huffed before she asked, "Where is it? I want a word with it."

Josh glanced up and chuckled. "You want a word with a cat?"

"It's not...," she started, then stopped and sighed. "What's the use? You won't believe me anyway. Take me to jail."

When she held her hands out in front of her, Alex shot me a quick glance before he asked, "Where's your sister?"

"She's the black cat."

We all stared at her. I was the first to ask, "She's the cat?"

Frieda rolled her eyes. "She's a witch who can turn into her familiar."

"Yeah? And I'm Santa Claus." Alex pulled out his handcuffs. "This stash will get me a promotion and an early retirement."

Since we'd dealt with witches before, I wasn't as quick to dismiss her claim. So far, I hadn't seen anything to convince me Frieda was for real. Tarot cards didn't count.

But I also had no reason not to believe her.

"Would you like me to bring Lucky to the station?" I asked as my gaze fell on Ralston's arm. The dark stain on his sleeve had spread as though he had a fresh injury that reopened in his struggles with Frieda.

"Only if you keep us in separate rooms," Frieda insisted.

I forgot about Ralston as I raised my eyebrows. What kind of cat lady wouldn't want to be reunited with one of her feline babies?

Cuffing her, Alex handed her off to Ralston. "Take her to an interrogation room. I'll bring Dash and the cat as soon as we're done here."

"Me?" I kept my brows lifted.

Josh flashed a grin as he and his partner continued to catalog the items in the cupboard. I kept a close eye on them both.

"The cat likes you," Alex reminded me. "It might be easier on everyone else if you were there to comfort it."

Frieda snorted. "My sister's always been more partial to girls than men, especially bleached blondes."

I grimaced as Alex's mic crackled. A man announced, "Send forensics to the backyard. We found something you'll want to see."

Everyone in the room fell eerily silent. Ralston stiffened. Frieda scowled. Josh met my gaze and seemed concerned at how I'd react.

"Josh, stay with the stuff in the cupboard. Ralston, you and Frieda stay here. Dash, keep an eye on all of them. Jake and I'll be right back." Alex touched my shoulder on the way by. Did he know something I didn't?

The moment the back door closed, Ralston whipped out his gun and turned it on Josh. "Put everything in the bag. No funny business, or I'll put a bullet in both of you."

"You don't want to do that, buddy," Josh said softly. "You need medical attention for those cuts you got from Dash's window."

Now things made sense. They were partners, which was why Ralston was with Alex, and why he and Freida kept having furtive conversations.

Frieda had slipped out of Alex's handcuffs and handed them to me. "Sure, we do. Just play nice and no one will get hurt."

"How did you...?" I started to ask, then noticed Josh give a small shake of his head. Whatever Alex knew, Josh was already in on. My gaze darted back to the passports as I played along. "Ah. The witch thing."

"You're a smart cookie," she said. "Too bad you're on the wrong team. I could use someone like you."

"Just like you used your sister?" I asked.

Josh cleared his throat as he emptied the jewels and cash from the cupboard, then raised the bag.

Ralston winced as he took it. Backing away toward the front door with a tight grip on Frieda's arm, the bag, and the gun. "Pleasure doing business with you."

Josh followed them with his camera clicking.

"Are you crazy? He'll shoot you."

He continued to take photos as Alex and the other officers surrounded Ralston and Frieda on the front porch with weapons drawn. The reporters went into a frenzy.

Ralston dropped everything and put up his hands.

Frieda wasn't about to go to jail easily. She made a break for it, shoving Alex aside and running toward the backyard. I dodged Josh and leaped over the stair rail to race after her without a second thought.

Until I hit the ground, and a sharp pain shot from my ankle right up my leg. Ignoring the twinge, I raced after the cat lady and tackled her to the ground near a rolled-up piece of moldy carpeting. The smell of decay barely registered as I sat on her back until one of Alex's backups took over.

By that point, I was seeing stars.

Someone draped an arm across my back and asked if I was okay, which was the last thing I remembered.

* * *

The nurses at the hospital gave me three stamps on the custom card they'd made for me. I suppose my first broken bone of the year—and my spectacular tackle with a broken ankle—was worthy of a free foot-long hot dog at Ricardo's food truck regardless of being two stamps short. Someone had stapled on an extra coupon for free fries and a drink.

Who was I to turn down sympathy food?

"I still can't believe that woman killed her sister, and my rookie was her accomplice," Alex said, as he helped me settle on my couch.

"What gave it away? The bloody shirt sleeve?" I asked, before my phone dinged.

"Saw you on the news," Rob Gwynn texted. *"You're a hero. How's the ankle?"*

"Painful. It earned me a free foot-long and sympathy from Alex. Lucky will be happy to get cuddles."

"Rob?" Alex asked.

"Yeah."

He flashed a pained smile as he set a small bag on the table next to me. "Here's the rest of your dinner. I'll leave out a can of food for Lucky and put the rest on the cupboard. Call me if you need anything."

"I will. Thanks."

"Who's Lucky?" Rob asked.

I chuckled as Alex opened a can and set it near the water bowl. Once he gave a wave and locked the front door behind him, I replied to Rob, *"Me. I have painkillers. Going to sail off with Jimmy now. Chat later. Night."*

I set my phone on the table and ignored the next two pings. I closed my eyes and enjoyed the purrs from the cat who reeked of kitty pate and Jimmy who crooned about—

When my phone pinged for a third time, I opened one eye, then waved a hand to ignore it. Lucky turned a circle on my stomach before settling on top of me. The phone pinged two more times. Finally, I relented and reached over to check the messages.

"Hey, it's Josh. Alex gave me your number, so I could check up on you."

Warmth spread through various parts of my body, starting at my chest. I wasn't sure if it was from the cat or some weird feeling that hearing from Josh had triggered.

"Wondered if you wanted to go for a jog on the beach in the morning," he said. I scowled, then read, *"Kidding! Feel better soon. Text me if you get bored."*

He followed the series of messages with a video of my leap off the porch and the ensuing tackle. *"The kids love this one as much as the llama video."*

After sending him a laugh emoji, I returned the phone to the table. As I closed my eyes, Lucky began to purr as Jimmy Buffett crooned about Monday. I had a feeling I'd see Josh again before long. I'd also see a lot more kooks now that another video of me was going viral.

- The End -

JOKER'S WILD

DIANE BATOR

DASH ALLMAN MYSTERIES BOOK

Jokers Wild

Dash Allman PI, Book 6

Diane Bator

Escape With a Writer Publishing

It was highly improbably that I'd meet Gumdrop the Drama Llama again in my lifetime—or even his. Yet there he was prancing alongside Daisy the goat in the annual Joker's Day Parade. My heart raced. By the time I looked around for people to hide behind, I was too late.

Gumdrop was heading toward me at a full trot. The bells on his colorful costume jingled as he let out a loud cry, took aim, then fired.

A wad of llama spit landed smack dab on my chest. In the exact same spot as when we'd first met on the beach before Christmas.

I groaned.

Gumdrop collapsed next to the curb.

Farmer Henry shouted as he stormed toward us, "Oh, for pity's sake! Get up. How many times do I have to tell you you're not a fainting goat?"

Daisy nudged Gumdrop, who rolled to his feet and winked at me. Apparently, we were still friends despite his repeated sniper attacks.

Phones waved in the air all around me,. Once again, my adventures with that darn llama would go viral. Maybe I should walk alongside Gumdrop and Daisy handing out business cards. Jobs as a private investigator dried up since my sudden online popularity as a llama whisperer.

"There you are, Dash," a voice called out.

Josh Marley, followed by a gaggle of squawking kids, beelined toward me. While Josh was a handsome, single, crime scene investigator who made my knees weak, I was in no hurry to meet the kids he coached at the community center. In fact, I'd gone so far out of my way to avoid it that I'd invented excuses such as cholera and measles. Oh, and my personal favorite, Gumdrop escaped, and I needed to go into protective custody. It seemed that one wasn't far off.

Since I'd already been spit on by the best, I might as well face the pre-teens head on. What's the worst they could do?

"Guys, this is my friend, Dash—," he started.

One kid's eyes grew wide. "Hey, you're the lady with the llama that Santa chased down the beach."

Suddenly, everyone around us buzzed with tales of which part of the Santa chase they liked the best. Gumdrop loping at full tilt across the sand, me hanging onto his harness for dear life with my feet floundering to touch the ground, or Santa Claus huffing and puffing behind us followed by a flock of screaming kids and parents.

The pre-teen voices were lost to a barrage of vocal pyrotechnics behind me as the next float appeared. I turned to see a man dressed in pointy-toed shoes and a black and red sequined jester suit hanging upside down from the hand of a gigantic papier mâché king. The statue itself was impressive. Twenty feet tall with a robe adorned with red and white roses, a bejeweled crown, glittering rings, and a red diamond on its chest.

When the man didn't perform any acrobatic twists or moves, a woman pointed and screamed, "He's dead!" bringing everyone else to an abrupt silence. The marching band stopped as though frozen in time. Three clowns ceased handing out balloons and candy. Volunteers along the route gawked.

A police officer ran in front of the cab of the truck with one palm up and the other hand on his holster. The jester swung forward as the truck pulling the float lurched to a stop, then swung back, hitting his head on the target on the king's belly.

"What's going on?" a kid asked, tugging on my arm. His small hands left a sticky spot near my wrist.

From the purple of the joker's face, I'd say he'd been dead for a while. Not something I wanted to announce to a flock of squawking kids.

"That does not look good," Josh voiced my thoughts. "Maybe I should take the kids for ice cream."

"No way," one of the kids said. "I wanna see the body."

Another boy agreed. "If your friend's a real detective, I wanna help her solve the case. Maybe since you're a forensics guy, you can help."

"I can help?" Josh asked. "Gee, thanks."

Suddenly, there was a cacophony of voices shouting, "Me, too." "I wanna help." "I have a note pad." "Can I check for the pulse?"

We all turned to stare at the little guy with the sticky fingers and the blue hat.

He shrugged. "What? I like crime shows. I wanna be a cop when I grow up."

I shook my head. "The police are on the case. We need to stay out of their way."

A chorus of "Aww" went up before another voice called out, "Hey, Dash. Get over here." Alex Carson, one of the heavier cops in question and long-time friend, waved me toward the float.

The kids cheered, running ahead of me and Josh. I wanted to find my arch nemesis, Gumdrop, and ride away from the whole scene. No such luck. The kids were swarming all over the case and I was stuck with them.

Alex shook his head before he asked, "What did you do now, Dash, adopt a Little League team?"

I pointed to Josh. "They're his."

When Alex raised his eyebrows, Josh clarified, "I'm their basketball coach."

The boy with a blue hat chuckled. "Did you really think he'd have nine ten-year-old kids of his own?"

"Or that he'd even have kids," another said. "He can't even keep a goldfish alive."

Good thing none of them knew about my history with houseplants. I caught the flare of red in Josh's cheeks as he muttered, "I'll take them for ice cream."

"But we want to help solve the murder," the blue hat kid announced.

"Ice cream, Crash," Josh repeated.

Crash—the runt of the litter—stood his ground, his jaw tightening as he folded his arms across his skinny chest. "Nuh-uh. I'm staying with Dash. Our names even rhyme."

I rolled my eyes. How did I keep attracting troublemakers? Probably because I was trouble. Karma really was a—

"Dash, I need you to do a coffee run," Alex said. "This is going to be a long night. Not only do we need to go over every inch of this float, but we'll need to redirect traffic for several hours."

"Coffee? No way!" Crash and I spit out in unison. The kid and I looked at each other in surprise, then grinned. Just like that I was stuck with another stray. At least he wasn't a llama, a goat, or a houseplant.

Josh shook his head. "You're supposed to stay with me until we get back to the community center."

Crash took his defiant stance once more, this time adding a glare that could've melted a snowman in a snowstorm. "And miss out on all the action? Are you kidding me?"

I let the two of them argue while I waited for Alex's coffee order. In the meantime, I took a quick photo of the body, noting there was something rectangular attached to the forehead of his mask. Then I glanced up the street to where several other officers questioned witnesses. Most of them likely saw the same thing we did. A joker dangling like a yo-yo from the hand of a papier mâché statue.

A tall man in a Harlequin costume darted along the sidewalk behind the antsy crowd and far away from the police. The way he glanced around as he moved made me think he had more than a little to hide.

Leaving Josh, Alex, and the kids behind, I dodged through the crowd after the bedazzled clown. Thankfully, he was tall enough for me to not lose sight of him as parade goers folded lawn chairs, tossed garbage to one side, and grumbled about missing the rest of the parade.

The fact a man was dead didn't seem to bother anyone.

As Harlequin glanced around, I ducked behind an elderly couple with a large umbrella. He turned left up the next street. By the time I swung around the corner, he was gone.

"Fish sticks," I growled, stomping my foot. I stood on the sidewalk glancing from door to door while I hoped for a clue.

"I'll bet he went into the warehouse," a little voice spoke beside me.

I spun around and managed not to lash out a fist in surprise. "What are you doing here, Crash?"

"When you snuck after that suspicious looking clown, I followed. If I would've—"

"Josh will be furious with both of us. Me, mostly, because I'm supposed to be the grown up."

Crash grinned. "You like him, don't ya?"

"I barely know him. You need to go back to the float with the others. Go for ice cream or whatever it is kids do these days."

He shook his head. "Nah. It's more fun hanging out with you."

"How do you know? You don't even know me."

"No, but I've seen your videos a hundred times each. The one of Santa chasing you and the llama down the beach is the best. I also like the one of you tackling that old lady. Those are way cool."

"Oh, great." I sighed, about to chastise him again when I spotted a piece of fabric on a nail next to a narrow door that led into the warehouse.

"What is it?" Crash asked. "Did you find him?"

Rather than admit the kid was right, I held up one hand. "You need to stay here. I'll be back in a minute."

Crash pressed his chest against my hand. "Uh-uh. I'm your back-up."

"You're ten."

He frowned. "You got a better option, Toots?"

Scrunching the front of his shirt in my fist and pulling him closer, I said, "If you ever call me Toots again, I'll tie you to the llama's belly and chase him into the ocean."

"Deal." He grinned.

This kid was going to drive me nuts. Since Josh and the rest of his ducklings had yet to appear, I took the kid by one sticky hand as we headed toward the door. "If anyone asks, we're looking for a washroom."

Crash pumped a fist in the air. "Yes!"

I took a photo of the fabric, then unhooked it from the doorway and stuck it in my pocket. Turning the knob, I pushed the door open and held up a finger warning Crash to be quiet as we stepped into the warehouse.

We both froze when we heard voices. Two men argued somewhere ahead in the semi-darkness. Crash's eyes practically bugged out of his elfin face. Keeping low, we snuck past a float identical to the one carrying the king statue.

"Why did they need two floats?" he whispered.

Just as confused, I shook my head and hushed him as we crawled beneath the float. We both peeked through the glittering streamer skirt on the other side of the trailer bed.

"Why didn't you tie Eight to the statue like I told you to?" a man shouted.

The Harlequin faced us but wore enough make-up I couldn't tell who he was. "I tried. The driver took off so fast I fell off into the foam gold under the king. I couldn't get back up without everyone seeing me, so I just stayed put until it stopped."

"Did anyone see you come here?"

"Don't think so," he said, rubbing his chin hard enough to take off some of the make-up off his reddish-blonde stubble. "I kept checking behind me."

There was a tense silence before the man with the gruff voice asked, "Did you at least get it?"

Crash looked at me and whispered, "Get what?"

I wrapped one arm around him and covered his mouth just as one of the large doors began to roll up. At that moment, a buzz came from my pocket. Crash and I stared at each other wide-eyed before I muted my phone.

On the other side of the glittery trailer skirt, a white panel truck rolled into the warehouse. The door closed before he'd even parked and turned off the engine. The sudden silence made my ears ring. The driver's door opened and a short man in sequined pants and a black hoodie hopped out.

I narrowed my eyes when I recognized Dog Chaney, the guy who sold wooden tables, bowls, and clocks at the local market. I thought for sure that rat would be in jail by now. "Oh, no."

"What in thundering circuses happened out there? Nobody was supposed to find the body until after the parade, not halfway through it," Dog barked. His voice rasped like he had a cold.

"You know him?" Crash whispered as the vertically challenged man raged.

I nodded, texting our location to Alex as I hid the phone behind Crash, so no one noticed the screen light.

"Where is it?" Dog finally asked.

The other two men exchanged guilty glances. After a couple minutes of silence, the shorter man stomped his foot. "Are you telling me you killed him before you got my diamonds back?"

As Crash met my gaze, we both mouthed, "Diamonds?"

"I tried to search his pockets but that's when he fell and—"

"You were supposed to tie him to the king's staff. No one was supposed to... I can't believe I hired you two nitwits. Get out of here. We'll meet tomorrow once I sort this mess out. In the meantime, you two knuckleheads better find those diamonds, or we're all dead men."

Dog stalked toward the truck. When the large door opened, he backed out and drove up the street away from both the police and the stalled parade.

The other two men started toward the float we lurked beneath. My chest tightened and I tensed, ready to make a run for it if they started the truck. Before the door could close, a large, white figure stepped inside.

"Oh. Crap," I muttered.

Gumdrop gave a loud, "Mwah". This time, rather than faint, the llama charged toward the two men. They scattered to either end of the warehouse. A short time later, both were led back to the float by uniformed police officers.

"You can come out now, Dash," Alex announced.

Releasing sigh of relief, Crash and I crawled out through the trailer's streamer skirt. Instantly, both men began to jabber about their innocence and insisted the kid and I were trespassing. Neither had any idea who we were or how we got inside the warehouse.

"Care to explain?" Josh appeared behind Alex. His glare darted from me to Crash and back again.

Before I could speak, Crash blurted out, "We were looking for a washroom."

"Mwah," Gumdrop said, this time he spit at me and dropped to the floor.

Crash burst into laughter. "Cool! Did you see that?"

"Too many times to count," I replied. "Get up, Gumdrop. You shouldn't be here either."

Alex shrugged. "He broke loose and was on his way here before you texted. Seems he knew you were in trouble. What a surprise. At least we got the bad guys and you're not in any new videos. You two can both go home."

"But what about the boss?" Crash asked.

When Alex raised his eyebrows, I nodded and added, "Dog Chaney hired them. Something about missing diamonds. Apparently, the dead guy had them last and whoever killed him didn't get them."

"We searched his pockets," Alex said. "He wasn't carrying anything. Not even identification."

"One of the men called him Eight." I met Josh's gaze. "No ID? Does that seem strange to you?"

"Maybe he was worried about a wallet showing under that outfit," Alex suggested.

"Maybe."

Crash walked over to Gumdrop who had rolled to sitting and eyed him warily. "You like Dash too, huh?"

Rather than spit at him, Gumdrop touched his snout to Crash's cheek. When Crash stroked the llama's neck, Gumdrop made a cat-like purr. Traitor.

"Can I ride the llama?" Crash asked.

We all chorused, "No!"

* * *

For most of my cases, I'd relied on my wits, my charm, and sheer dumb luck. My father always amused dinner guests by saying that if it wasn't for dumb luck, I'd have no luck at all.

Two hours in, I realized I was over my head with this case and needed to consult with an expert. What did a single, thirty-something like me know about diamonds? I'd never owned one. Cubic zirconia jewelry from my parents was the closest I'd ever come. Even though my mom owned several large sparklers, mostly apology gifts from my father.

I locked my front door and turned on the computer before I grabbed a soda. When a loud meow came from the bedroom, I paused to put some cat food in the dish for Lucky, the cat who'd moved in with me a month earlier. So far, he'd fared well. I suspected he'd found the occasional rodent.

Thankfully, the internet kept a wide range of information right at my fingertips, and I didn't have to think much. I looked up diamond sizes, colors, cuts, and local robberies.

It even showed me diamond playing card tarot meanings.

The King of Diamonds was a shrewd man who executed deals and grew wealth with good decisions.

The Queen of Diamonds was a business woman who enjoyed wealth, luxury, and abundance. Wouldn't we all?

The Joker was the Fool. It represented hidden agendas and how things weren't always as they seemed.

Within the hour, I was completely immersed in all things diamond related and barely heard my phone ring. "Dash Allman, PI."

"Dashiell, I'd like to hire you."

Normally, those words thrilled me. The way my mom said them sent a shock wave through my body. "Has Uncle Scott run off again?"

My uncle, an alcoholic gambler with an eye for women with money, tended to latch on to Sugar Mamas on a regular basis. I'd usually track him down in Las Vegas or Atlantic City under a roulette table with a bottle of something cheap.

"Not this time. He's trying to help," she told me.

"Help with what?"

"Someone stole my diamonds."

A lightbulb flickered above my head as another puzzle piece floated by just out of my reach. Could those be among the diamonds Dog was looking for?

After giving Lucky some overdue cuddles and a kitty treat, I hopped on my moped—the only form of transportation I could afford—and puttered out to the mansion my parents shared with six dogs, a huge cage filled with noisy birds, and a herd of horses.

The horses they kept in elaborate barns with air-conditioning. The rest of the menagerie held court in the solarium, which stood where my bedroom once was. Back when the house was a three-bedroom farmhouse and not a huge pink stucco eyesore. The few times I did stay over, I used the Pink Room at the opposite end of the house, which now boasted six bedrooms, each with a private bath, and a maze of other rooms I doubted they ever used.

Story of my life. From Rich Kid to Beach Bum all in one swift kick out the door at sixteen. That's a whole other story.

My mother's taste in décor had slid from Farmhouse Chic to something out of a Bond villain's private island lair. Gold, gaudy, and adorned with jungle animals. Her mid-life crisis was almost as bad as my father's. He was the one responsible for the multitude of noisy birds in the gilded cage and the horses.

Did I mention my mystery-loving Mom also ran a high fashion magazine? Having a beer-drinking, tattooed daughter who worked with slimeballs and deadbeats didn't exactly keep me in her good graces on a regular basis. Especially when I ended up in the emergency room now and then. My last broken bone earned me a free, pity hot dog from Ricardo's food truck, courtesy of the emergency room nurses who were already laying bets on when I'd show up next.

I cleared my throat and tried to sound professional. "When did you notice the diamonds missing?"

"Last night when we got back from the Simmons' party," my mother said. "I took off my emerald earrings, the ones with twin diamonds. When I went to put them away, I saw..." She burst into tears. "I was so awful."

I tried to maintain my cop voice as I'd heard Alex and Rob use far too many times. "Did you call the police?"

My parents exchanged scared glances. I guessed bringing in the police was out of the question, but why?

Already frustrated, I tried a different tact. "Did you notice anything out of the ordinary? A door or window open that you know you'd closed. Dresser drawers ransacked or dumped on the floor." When they stared blankly, I added, "Signs that someone was looking for valuables."

My father's face flushed. "Should we have looked?"

For most people, searching the house for an intruder, or at least an open door or window, would've been a natural instinct. Right up there with calling the police. My parents lacked certain basic instincts. Like nurturing, for one.

"What did you do then?" I asked.

"Washed up and went to bed," my mother replied with a shrug. "We couldn't call our insurance agent until this morning anyway."

Every insurance company I'd ever dealt with—one, to be exact—wanted a police report. Even though the police found a murder weapon in my house, making it a secondary crime scene, the insurance agent was less than helpful with regards to my broken window. Until my landlord got involved.

Funny how connected people were in our community. My landlord knew both he insurance agent's wife—and his girlfriend.

"Did they ask for a police report?" I asked.

Once more my parents shot each other those weird glances. I had half a mind to either leave or question them separately. And to call Alex Carson.

"Why don't you show me where you kept the diamonds?"

My parents remained seated. There was that look again.

That time, I huffed and felt like I was talking to two guilty toddlers. "Do you actually want my help, or is this some kind of joke?"

They were saved from further questions as my father's phone rang. He leaped to his feet and left my mother stuck with my disapproving glare.

When my father's voice dropped to a hushed whisper, I frowned. "Who's your insurance company?"

"Berkley," she said too quickly. "Would you like to see the scene of the crime now?"

"That would be helpful."

The name Berkley rang a bell, but I couldn't recall why. For the moment, I followed her up the winding staircase with brass palm tree spindles that supported a brass railing. Their bedroom took up a third of the second floor and had a huge marble ensuite with a jacuzzi tub big enough for four people, plus a two-foot-tall brass elephant at the foot of the bed.

I refused to ask why they had either.

My mother walked over to a portrait of she and my father all dressed up in gown and tuxedo from some fundraiser or another. She took the photo off the wall to reveal a ten-by-ten inch safe I'd never seen before.

Facing me, she turned her finger in a circle. A signal for me to turn around.

"Seriously? The diamonds are gone. Who am I going to tell?" I asked.

She scowled, then tapped her foot on the plush gray carpet. "Turn around."

"Fine." I relented and turned, finding myself face to face with my reflection in a floor-to-ceiling mirror. Either my mother didn't realize I could still see her, or she doubted my abilities to figure out the combination by watching her spin the dial in reverse.

She spun the lock to thirty-eight, then twenty-nine, then to fifty-seven and opened it before announcing, "You can turn around now."

I closed my eyes, making a show of facing her before opening them.

As far as safes went, it was the smallest I'd seen lately. Definitely, the emptiest. I hesitated for a minute to collect my thoughts before asking her to leave the room.

Panic filled her face. "Why?"

"Technically, it's a crime scene," I explained. "Since you didn't call the police, I'm first on scene and need to try to preserve any evidence and examine the room for clues."

She looked doubtful.

I didn't blame her. She always seemed to know when I was lying though my teeth. This time—luckily for me—she bought it.

The second she left the room, I sighed, then locked the door and put a chair in front of it for good measure. Since the elephant weighed more than me, and I wasn't going to touch it with a ten-foot bamboo pole for anything, the chair would suffice.

My parents were up to something, and I had a gut feeling it involved Ian and Sophia Simmons, although I couldn't explain why. Not until I opened my father's night table drawer and found a business card for Berkley Insurance.

Ian Simmons was one of their agents. In fact, he was my parents' agent.

Mental head slap.

I'd bet a box of donuts that's who'd called my father.

Beneath Ian's business card was a playing card. The nine of diamonds, which seemed like an odd thing for him to keep in the night table, but to each his own. With my stomach churning, I snapped photos rather than disturbing anything, just because the two cards bothered me.

I searched the drawers and cabinets afraid of what I might find. Not so much about things that might incriminate either of my parents, more like things they might use on a more...intimate level. They were still my parents and that childhood ick factor was still a thing.

No diamonds. No weapons. Nothing incriminating. Not even any adult toys. Satisfied my parents were telling the truth, I moved the chair back in place and decided to have a face-to-face chat with Ian

Simmons. Maybe he could enlighten me with regards to the diamonds and my parents' insurance policy.

* * *

I opened my eyes and stared at the bright blue sky. Palm fronds waved in front of my face as though making sure I was okay. I never should've tried scaling the Simmons' trellis to get to the study on the second floor when no one answered the door. Who knew it was old wood painted to look fresh and white?

"Are you okay?" a voice called out.

The gardener, Franz Hensel, hadn't changed since I was twelve. Still gray haired and weathered, he carried the same rusty rake in one hand.

As he crouched over me, I gave a groan making sure to sound pathetic as I asked, "Who am I?"

"You're that snot-nosed trouble maker from up the street. Dash Allman," he said. "What're you doing here?"

I stared wide-eyed. "That depends. Where am I?"

Hensel shook his head, then hauled me to my feet. "I'll take you inside for a cold drink. After that you either leave or I call the cops."

"Why would you do that?" I didn't have to fake being light-headed and staggering.

He grabbed me around the shoulders to steer me around a wheelbarrow. "Because the last time you were here, you made trouble for us all. My mama still thinks I'm a criminal because the police questioned me about stealing the Simmons' diamonds back when you were a nosy kid."

I tried hard not to look surprised that his mother was still alive. When I was a kid, I already thought he was in his seventies. I guessed Hensel was one of those people who didn't age well. That, or his mother was a vampire.

He led me into the kitchen through the back door and sat me at the breakfast nook. Jenna Simmons and I used to hang out in that kitchen until her parents decided I was a bad influence on her. I was twelve at the time and doing surveillance on their house.

"Here." Hensel set a glass of tap water on the table in front of me, then popped a beer open for himself. "Drink up and get out before Mr. Simmons sees you."

"He's home?"

Hensel's face darkened. "You still ask a lot of questions, don't you?"

I wanted to remind him that I was a detective, but that would only get me thrown out faster. Sipping the lukewarm water, I jumped when a phone rang across the kitchen. Who had a landline anymore?

Hensel stared at it but didn't move until no one else had answered it by the third ring. He lumbered across the kitchen and snatched up the receiver. "Simmons Residence."

The moment he turned his back, I shot out of the kitchen and into the hall that led to the front foyer. Nothing had changed but the layer of dust. If anyone else was home, they were awfully quiet.

I raced up the carpeted stairs to the second-floor study hoping to confront Ian Simmons if he was there. If not, I'd search for clues as to what his business had to do with my mom's diamonds.

Ian Simmons sat behind his desk. He didn't make a sound when I entered the room. Nor did he look at me. Blood trickled down the right side of his face as he stared vacantly toward the patio doors I'd attempted to reach via the trellis.

"You'd better not be up here, Dash, or I'm calling the police," Hensel huffed and puffed up the stairs behind me.

When he burst into the room behind me he stopped short and gave a gasp that made me think he was having a heart attack. His gaze met mine and his lips moved in silence, either in prayer or cursing.

"Be sure to ask for Alex Carson, I told him. "And tell them your boss is dead. You should use the phone downstairs. The police will have to dust the office for prints. Since you already used that one a few minutes ago, your prints are on it."

He nodded, then backed out of the room.

I reached into my pocket for the gloves I'd brought. This was as good a time as any to search Ian Simmons' office, since it wasn't like anyone could stop me. What did he have to do with the missing diamonds and the parade float? If the two were even connected.

My first thought was to check for a pulse, but I was too squeamish. From the hue of his lips, I was likely far too late. Instead, I stood on the opposite side of his desk to peer at his day planner. It wasn't as easy to translate upside down as I'd hoped. I pulled out my phone, snapped a few photos, and intended to be out of the study long before the police arrived.

A loud scream behind me kiboshed that plan.

I turned to see Jenna Simmons.

A wide-eyed little boy stood beside her. He asked, "Dash? What are you doing here?"

Crash. As much as I wanted to roll my eyes and yell, "Of course you're here." I didn't have the chance.

Before I could speak, Jenna shrieked, "You killed my father!"

"No, she didn't, Miss Jenna," Hensel said, coming up the stairs to my rescue. "He was like that when we came to see him."

My eyebrows did a little jump. Why was Hensel sticking up for me?

"Dash wouldn't kill anyone," Crash announced. "Right, Dash?"

"Right." I nodded.

Hensel herded us all down to the livingroom. Now that there were witnesses, any chance of me doing any further investigating was long gone. I followed them down the stairs with my head bowed like a condemned prisoner.

"Can I show Dash my room?" Crash asked, halting the somber procession.

"No, you may not," Jenna snapped, shooting me a steely glare.

The boy grabbed my arm as we reached the bottom of the stairs and nodded toward the front door. "Me and Dash will wait outside for the cops. She knows them all anyway."

My face warmed as Jenna shot me yet another scowl. "And just how do you know that, young man?"

His eyes grew wide. "Uh. Josh told us. Dash was the girl in that llama video I told you about."

Before Jenna or Hensel could stop us, Crash hustled me out the front door. Rather than sit on the front step as stated, he dragged me around to the back of the house below the study.

"Oh, wow! Two dead guys in one weekend. What are the odds?" Crash asked. "Hey, do you see that? The trellis is broken. I'll bet that's how the killer got in."

I picked up my sunglasses, which were still lying on the grass. "Actually, that was me trying to sneak in. Then the wood broke and Hensel found me on the ground."

Crash gawked at me for a long second before bursting into laughter. He finally stopped long enough to ask if I was okay, then added, "Wish I'd been able to video tape that one."

"Gee, kid, thanks for your concern."

"Did you see anything?" he asked.

"Just stars."

The kid smirked.

"I guess I ruined any chance of finding evidence out here," I told him, gazing up at the second-floor window.

He kicked at the broken pieces of trellis. "Did you at least see anything inside before Mom screamed."

"Mom?" I asked.

Jenna Simmons—the Golden Girl—had a kid?

While she did have a string of boyfriends all through high school, I'd never heard any pregnancy rumors. Giving my head a quick shake, I remembered Ian's day planner. "Maybe I did see something. Let's see if you can make sense of these."

We sat on the grass between the house and the pool while I pulled up the photo of Ian's day planner and held out my phone. "Do these initials mean anything to you?"

Crash enlarged each one, then shook his head. "Nope."

I'd have to print the photo once I got home to see what I could decipher.

"What's that?" he asked, pointing to one corner of the picture. "I'll bet it's from that guy in the white truck we saw."

One of Ian's hands was in the shot. Between his fingers was a scrap of cloth with sequins. It was the same color as Dog's costume and the only solid hunch we had.

As sirens wailed toward the Simmons' place, I crossed my fingers Alex was with them, so I'd have less explaining to do. We meandered around the corner, then I froze.

Crash walked a few feet ahead before looking back at me in concern. "You okay?"

Alex got out of the driver's side, while Rob Gwynn emerged from the passenger side. Rob and I had dated off and on since the murder of one of my clients. I hadn't seen him since Christmas due to his back surgery. From what I heard he wasn't allowed to skateboard anymore. Ever.

"Dash Allman. What a surprise," Rob said. He'd put on a few pounds since I last saw him, but still resembled the statue of David only with dark hair and mahogany eyes.

"Ahem. Are you gonna introduce me?" Crash asked, his elbow digging into my hip.

Before I could say anything, Alex announced, "Careful, Rob. This is the Dash and Crash Show."

"This is the kid from the parade?" Rob asked.

I could feel my reputation as a P.I. took yet another steep nosedive. No wonder I hadn't seen Rob in months. I was notorious.

Rob shrugged. "I suppose we'd better put them in separate cars. For safety's sake."

Crash let out a yell and ran into the house as the two men chuckled.

"That wasn't funny, guys," I told them.

Alex patted my shoulder. "We're just trying to save the kid from a life of crime fighting."

"Seriously? Most people are more concerned with kids falling into a life of crime."

"Yeah, except we know you," Rob said.

Alex cleared his throat then met my gaze before he asked, "How did you break into the house before finding the body?"

"I didn't." Not after the trellis broke, anyway. "I was invited."

Hensel appeared in the doorway. "Are you gentlemen coming inside or jawing out here with the trespasser?"

So much for having my back. Hensel threw me under the proverbial bus.

Rob nudged me toward the house. "Invited, huh?"

I refused to answer him, or acknowledge Jenna, who immediately accused me of killing her father.

Crash jumped in front of me facing her with his hands on his narrow hips. "Did you hear a gunshot?"

No one replied.

Jenna sighed. "I did hear a noise outside my window."

"Could've been a bird," Crash replied.

Hensel cleared his throat. "Or a private detective trying to climb the trellis."

"Up or down?" Rob asked.

I didn't like his implication. When had I become the enemy?

When Alex asked Hensel to show them to the study, my shoulders sagged. Rob must've heard about my latest exploits with the cat lady. He must've learned about Crash and I hiding under the parade float. And possibly about Josh.

From the top of the stairs, Rob gave a whistle. "Dash. You need to show us what you touched."

"Why? You already have my prints on file anyway," I muttered as I mounted the bottom stair.

Crash grabbed my arm. "Can I come?"

Until that moment, I never knew boys could bat their eyelashes like wistful girls. The kid was good at it. Just like Jenna when we were kids. It was one trait that always annoyed me, which made it easy for me to say, "No."

"No."

"Honey, come and sit with me," Jenna said. "I don't want to be alone."

His face fell.

"I'll fill you in later," I promised.

"Yeah. Sure. That's what all the adults say." The kid bowed his head.

It sounded like he'd been let down a lot by the grownups in his life just like I had. My phone dinged when I was near the study door.

"It's Crash. Send me the pic of the book."

I could, but did I want to involve him in a murder investigation? Entering the study, I ignored his request but wondered how he got my number to begin with. The farther I could keep him out of things, the better off we both were.

Rob stopped me at the door to hand me a pair of booties. "Did you come in through the balcony door?"

"No. I tried but the trellis broke. I landed on my back in the grass. Hensel brought me into the kitchen for a cold drink. When the phone rang, he answered it, and I came up to see Ian. He was already..."

"You're right. Good thing we already have your prints on file," Rob said, walking away to inspect the patio doors.

"Thanks for the vote of confidence. The only thing I got a look at was his day planner, which is written in some kind of code."

Alex handed me fresh gloves along with a "don't touch anything" warning. While the officers perused the crime scene, I took one more look at the top of Ian Simmons' desk. A file with the name Allman on the tab stuck halfway from beneath a red file folder. The initials D.C. jumped out at me. Was Dog Chaney another one of Ian's clients, or was that a cover for something more nefarious?

"Dash?" Alex asked.

"Huh?"

"I asked if you knew any of the names or places in his book."

Nudging the red folder over the Allman one, I peered over the list I'd snapped the photo of earlier.

"Bob. DHC. RA. CR@3pm. Dn 8pm Rd Pal," I read aloud. "Sounds like some kind of shorthand."

"Good guess, Nancy Drew," Rob muttered.

I bristled. Bad enough he seemed mad at me, but I had no idea why since I hadn't seen or heard from him in months aside from a text when I broke my ankle and appeared on the evening news tackling the cat lady. I sensed a showdown in our near future.

"You guys know how to throw the most lavish parties," Josh Marley, one of the forensics investigators, said from the doorway.

Another white suited tech strolled into the room already wearing gloves, booties, and protective glasses. She was a foot shorter than Josh's six feet, thin—even in the white suit—and wouldn't know a breakfast dog if she tripped over one. She gave a nod, then got to work. No smile. I already didn't like her.

Josh did a brief introduction, "Rob. Alex. Dash. This is Colleen."

Then he shooed us out of the room while they started tagging, photographing, and collecting evidence.

"Who's the kid?" Rob asked at the top of the stairs. "I heard he was with you at the parade yesterday."

"He's one of the kids Josh coaches at the community center. He's also Jenna Simmons' son."

Alex made a noise. "He's what?"

I lowered my voice. "I just found out, too. He lives here with his mom and his grandparents. I have a feeling he could help with Ian's code."

"Not to mention he seems sneaky enough to know everything that goes on around here," Rob said. "Kind of like you."

"Oh, you have no idea," Alex told him.

Rob flinched at his partner's tone, then asked, "So how do we question him without having to deal with Jenna?"

Unable to believe what I was about to say, I cleared my throat. "Why don't I hang out with him while you question Jenna and Hensel? I'm sure they both know more than they're letting on. I know Crash does."

"Divide and conquer?" Alex asked. "Might work. Besides, he already trusts you."

I suppressed a grin. "And he wants to help. Besides, I'd rather Crash not be in the room while they take his grandfather out. He's scarred enough already."

"Just don't leave the yard," Alex warned.

I held up my left hand. "Scout's honor."

Rob chuckled. "Wrong hand, Dash."

"Oh, like I was ever a scout."

Alex explained to Jenna how I'd keep an eye on Crash in the backyard while he and Rob questioned she and Hensel.

Her cheeks reddened, but she gave a nod. "Come give me a hug, Charlie."

"Charlie?" I grinned.

The boy sighed, his face red. "You promised to call me Crash, Mom."

Jenna kissed his cheek. "I know. Just be good for Dash, and don't leave the property. Either of you."

"We won't, Mom," he said.

We took a detour through the kitchen where he grabbed two sodas from the fridge and a bag of chips. Rather than hanging out on the patio furniture in the shade, he sat on the edge of the pool and dangled his legs in the water just like Jenna and I used to.

I imitated him, then nudged his arm. "Charlie, huh?"

"Don't start. What's your real name? Dorothy?"

"Dashiell."

He looked startled, then chuckled. "That's actually kinda cool."

"Only if you had a daughter you wanted to torture for the rest of her life."

Crash cracked open his root beer. "Too bad you got stuck with me,."

"Are you kidding? I volunteered to hang out with you. This is way better than staying inside to answer dumb questions. 'What are you doing here, Dash?' 'Why'd you climb up the trellis?' They always make me feel like the bad guy."

"Are you?"

"Nope. Are you?"

Crash chugged some of his soda, then belched. "No way. Hey, you didn't send me that picture."

"Ah. Right." After I sent it, I sat back to watch him study it and think.

"Rd Pal is the Red Palace Restaurant. He has lots of meetings there."

I sat up straighter. "He planned to meet someone there at eight o'clock tonight."

"Bob, DHC, RA, or CR?" he asked, then frowned. "Wait. It says three p.m. at CR. That must be another place. What time is it?"

I glanced at my phone. "One-thirty. Is there a place your grandpa went to that has the initials CR?"

Crash's eyes watered. "I called him Ian. He didn't like me calling him Grandpa."

"That's tough. What about your grandma?"

"Same. I call her Sophie. She plays cards with friends or meets them at the country club. Sometimes, she just takes off for rides alone in her convertible. If you ask me, I think she's got a boyfriend."

His comment caught me off guard as a sense of déjà vu pushed through me. The kid knew too much about everything. As though everyone forgot he was in the room. Crash was a lot like me as a kid.

Actually, he was a lot like me now.

"I'm sure the police will track her down," I said, trying to comfort him even though he didn't seem upset about any of the goings on.

"Okay." He stuffed a handful of chips into his mouth.

While Crash devoured the junk food, I took another look at the photos of the Jester hanging on the float, then the one of Ian's day planner. Something bothered me that I couldn't put a finger on. His office was impeccable, yet the desk was covered with file folders.

Then my gaze fell on the playing card.

Why hadn't I noticed the King of Diamonds sticking out of his breast pocket? Especially after seeing one stuck to the first body and another in my dad's nightside table. I zoomed in on the photo of the Jester. It was difficult to make out but the card he had appeared to be the Joker.

A Joker on the Jester. A Nine at my parents' house. Now a King in Ian's front pocket. Someone wasn't playing with a full deck.

"Do you know what the King of Diamonds means?" I asked.

Crumbs fell from Crash's mouth to float on the salt water. "Should I?"

"No, I guess not."

After a long minute, he faced me and asked, "Didn't the dead guy on the float have a Joker card?"

The kid was more observant than even I gave him credit for. I guessed that was why we got along. "Yes."

"Did Ian have a card? I didn't get to see."

Zooming in on Ian's pocket, I held out my phone. "This makes me wonder if there's a connection between the two, especially since Dog and his friend were talking about diamonds."

"But where did they get them?"

I had a couple hunches about that. Too bad I'd promised my parents I'd keep their privacy. I grinned. I'd only promised not to tell the police. No one said anything about a ten-year-old wannabe detective.

"There have been a lot of burglaries around here lately," Crash offered before I could volunteer my information. "Ian was talking to some guy on the phone this morning and telling him to relax. He doubted anyone would find the diamonds anyway. With the money the guy would get, he could take his wife on a trip or shopping for new jewelry."

A chill settled over me. The mysterious phone call my father took. It had to be. Would he end up being the next victim?

"Dash," Rob called out the backdoor. "I need you two back inside."

"Is he gonna cross-examine me?" Crash whispered.

"It's called interrogating, and probably."

"Dang. Will you come with me?"

I shrugged. "If I'm allowed to. Jenna...I mean, your mom, might not want me there."

"How come she doesn't like you?" he asked.

"I was a nosy kid, too."

We gathered our trash and walked past the shards of trellis. I was sure I spotted something out of the ordinary. A scrap of sequined cloth. Odd. If the trellis couldn't hold my weight, there was no way it would hold anyone else. Except maybe Crash, and I refused to entertain that thought. That narrowed the shooter down to a few thousand jokers running around town for the weekend who weighed less than a buck twenty.

I left the scrap for the forensics team to find and followed Crash inside. Jenna sat at the kitchen table with fresh mascara trails on her cheeks while she sipped a glass of white wine. Hensel leaned against the sink with a can of beer in one hand and his phone in the other. Both glanced up but neither spoke.

Crash flopped onto the couch across from Rob and Alex. He patted the seat beside him for me to sit before asking, "Who died now?"

Both men raised their eyebrows.

I draped my arm around Crash's neck and covered his mouth. "What do you say we use our ears, not our mouths? That's what good detectives do."

He nodded.

I removed my hand and came away with salt crystals from his chips. Wiping my hand on my shorts, I tried to focus on the questions but was too distracted thinking about my father's role in whatever mischief was going on. Why did he have Nine of Diamonds?

"Dash?" Crash nudged me.

Jumping, I said, "What?"

"You're not using your ears."

"Sorry. I was thinking about the playing cards."

Rob and Alex exchanged glances before Rob asked, "What do you know about the cards?"

I shrugged. "The Joker was on the guy we saw on the float. The King of Diamonds in Ian's coat pocket. They don't make sense."

Crash hopped to his feet. "Hey. The Joker was hanging off the King. Did the King on the float have a card or anything?"

"Good question. I'll take another look," Alex said, pulling out his phone.

I was positive he already knew the answer but was humoring us. When Alex held out a photo of the papier mâché king, minus the joker. Square on the King's chest was a diamond like the one on the cards. Inside the diamond were three progressively smaller diamonds. Just like a target. Precisely where the jester had hit his head when the truck stopped.

My breath caught in my throat.

"We need to go," Alex announced. "Come on, Dash. We'll give you a ride home."

Despite my moped being parked up the street at my parents' house, I nodded, then met Crash's gaze. "You have my number. Call me if you need anything."

He wrapped his arms around me. "I wish you could stay."

"You and your family need time together," I told him as I hugged him back. "I need to get cross-examined."

He smiled despite his tears. "You mean interrogated."

"Oh, I hope so," I whispered before following Rob and Alex to the squad car.

They sat me in the back seat like a criminal. None of us spoke as Alex drove away. Three blocks later, Alex glanced back at me and asked, "What do you know, Dash?"

"The guy on the float was a message but for who?"

"I'd say Ian," Rob said. "He had the King of Diamonds in his pocket."

"Except that we don't know if he was even at the parade," I reminded him. "And what do the cards represent? Do you think it's some street gang or criminal ring? There's been a lot of diamond thefts lately. Maybe they—"

Alex hit the brakes, stopping in the middle of the street. "What did you and the kid hear in the warehouse again?"

"Dog Chancy talked about missing diamonds. Maybe someone in their ring double-crossed him, and—"

"And now they're dead," Rob added. "But who would double cross him? The Joker or Ian Simmons?"

I kept my mouth shut and gazed out the window. After all, I had promised.

"Dash." Alex's voice held the edge of a warning. "Spill it."

Rob turned around to look at me as best he could. "Spill what?"

"She knows something, and if she doesn't tell us soon, she's not only going to be cross-examined she'll be held in contempt."

"We're not in court," I replied. "And I still have my Get Out of Jail Free card. The one you gave me for Christmas."

"Both of those can change fast," he warned.

Under duress, I told them about the call from my parents regarding their missing diamonds, finding the Nine of Diamonds in my father's drawer, and the call my dad took about the same time as the one Crash overheard Ian make. I also mentioned the file folders on Ian's desk for my parents and for Dog Chaney.

"What are you thinking?" Rob asked.

"That they're all involved in some kind of insurance scam. Someone steals the diamonds, the victims get paid off, and everyone's happy. I'll bet every person who had diamonds stolen recently are clients of Berkley Insurance. More specifically, Ian Simmons was their agent."

Rob pulled out his phone. "You'd better hope you're right."

"It's just a guess," I insisted.

"It's the best we have to go on," Alex said. "We need to go talk to your parents."

I shook my head feeling like I was twelve again. "Then you'd better put me in a jail cell for my own protection, or they'll strangle me for ratting them out."

As predicted, my parents, Gus and Mary Alice Allman, were less than thrilled when I showed up in the back of a police car yet again. Even in handcuffs, which the neighbors out doing yard work enjoyed.

"You told them?" my mom asked in a stage whisper.

"Hello. Handcuffs." I turned to show her.

She frowned. "Seriously, Alex? She's a trouble maker, but even you know she's relatively harmless."

"Relatively?" I squawked.

As Rob released me from the handcuffs, he whispered, "Play along. We need their full co-operation."

As if he needed to explain that. I sat in one of the tropical flowered wingback chairs while my parents huddled on the matching couch murmuring to each other.

"Tell us about the missing diamonds," Rob said, using his best bad cop voice.

While my father cringed, my mother flared her nostrils and glared at me. It was my father who filled them in on the details, even handing Alex a copy of the list of items stolen. Almost as though he'd expected the police to show up. Did he think I couldn't keep a secret, or had he expected someone in the ring to talk?

Then Rob dropped the bombshell about Ian Simmons, labeling his death a suicide. My father's left eyebrow twitched before he bowed his head.

"Suicide?" My mother shook her head. "I can't even imagine. How's Sophia doing?"

"Well, that's the other issue," Alex said. "Sophia Simmons is missing. I thought you might know where to find her."

"Why us?" my father asked.

Rob met my gaze with a quick glance. "You are neighbors. We thought you might be good friends as well."

Before they could respond, Alex cleared his throat. "What's the deal with the King of Diamonds?"

"What does all of this have to do with playing cards?" my mother asked.

My father began to cough. "I need water."

I didn't want to leave the room but stood to get him a glass. I froze when Alex asked, "Were you in an insurance scam with Ian Simmons?"

This time, my father coughed so hard he turned scarlet, then purple, before he gasped. "I don't...know what...you're talking about."

Sighing, I sat back down without getting him any water. "Just tell them the truth, they'll find out anyway. I found the Nine of Diamonds in your night table."

My father went from purple to gray. Seconds later, he caught his breath and began to regale us with the story. "Ian came to me with an idea to get money out of the insurance company. They were forcing him to retire after thirty-four years and cutting the pension they'd promised him. Seems there's a new punk who took over last year and he's been trimming the fat. Anyone who wanted to retire, was being shoved out the door with nothing to show for it."

My mother bowed her head and wiped away a tear. "It was awful. Sophia was at her wits end. They'd have to leave the country club and sell things to make ends meet."

"Ian came up with the Diamond Gang," my father announced, taking her hand. "He recruited some guys he knew to help."

"I'll need those names," Alex told him.

"I only know them by their code names. King, Queen, Jack, Ten, Nine, Eight, and Joker," he admitted.

Rob raised his eyebrows. "Interesting choices."

"Ian was King. I was Nine. Whenever we met, we wore masks."

"Jack is Dog Chaney," I said. "That's what they called him in the warehouse."

My father scowled and clenched his fists in his lap. I already knew too much.

"And the dead man on the float yesterday was Joker," Rob added.

"He couldn't be," my father said. "I saw Joker last night."

"Augustus," my mother snapped.

My back straightened. "So, you do know them."

"Not by name." He seemed to shrink a couple inches.

Alex handed him a notebook turned to a clean sheet. "Write down what you do know. Code names, real names, descriptions, everything."

My mother hugged a throw pillow. "I need a drink."

No one offered to get her one. We were all watching my father filling a page in Alex's small book. When he was done, I leaned closer to read.

King of Diamonds: Ian Simmons.

Queen: ?

Jack: truck driver, short guy, gruff voice. Since we already knew Dog Chaney was the Jack, I skipped to the next one.

Ten: tall, skinny guy, Franz?

Nine.

Here my father hesitated. He met my gaze before he sighed and wrote his name. Augustus Allman. I closed my eyes as a hollow sensation settled into my stomach. My father had just admitted to being a criminal.

Eight: Mitch Herrington.

Joker.

This time when he stopped, he lay the pen across the paper.

"What's wrong?" Rob asked.

"Gus values his life," my mother replied.

My eyes widened. "What does that mean?"

Bowing his head, my father sighed as he pressed the tips of his fingers together.

"Did he threaten you?" I asked.

"He threatened us all," my father told us. "Now Ian and Mitch are dead."

I frowned. "Mitch Herrington was the Joker on the float?"

"Only he's not the joker," my father admitted. "He was Eight. The card was a warning for the rest of us. So was the King. The real King statue was on the second float in the warehouse. I have no idea who made the one that ended up in the parade. The one with the target."

Alex took a closer look at the list. "So, either the Joker is planning to walk away with all the diamonds, or he's someone else's pawn. Who's Franz?"

"I'm not sure. Dog called him that once. Ian wanted us to stick to code names only, so no one could talk to each other."

"Or get killed," my mother added. "You, Franz, and Dog are next."

"Unless one of them is in cahoots with the killer," I told her.

"Cahoots?" Rob asked, meeting my gaze.

"It's a word."

"Yeah, I know, but..."

Alex held up a hand. "Enough, you two. Gus, when's the next meeting?"

"This afternoon at three. We're getting together at Dog's shop for the cash run."

My eyebrows jumped as if with little minds of their own. CR@3pm. Cash Run at three.

"Where's your mask?" Alex asked. "I'm going in your place."

My first impulse was to object. The Joker could kill him. Then my gaze fell on my father. Alex could wear body armor and have backup. My father would be a sitting duck.

* * *

Dog's shop was in an old garage outside of town. Alex parked in the lot, got out of my dad's silver Porsche, and looked around. He looked ridiculous in the Harlequin costume my father loaned him. Thankfully, they were about the same size. The wire he wore was so small it didn't show at all.

Rob parked several vehicles away with me secured in the backseat. By secured, I mean handcuffed for everyone else's safety.

"This isn't fair," I muttered for the tenth time since we'd left my parents' house.

He met my gaze in the mirror. "No, but this way you can't do something dumb like sneak into the back entrance or drug me."

"It was only one pill, and you were suffering."

"I was out for hours," Rob said, then radioed to make sure everyone was in place.

My heart raced as Alex adjusted his suit and strolled into the shop. He walked so much like my father it made me shiver.

"You're late," Dog barked over the speaker.

"Traffic," Alex growled.

"Let's get this over with," another man said. "The police are onto us."

I gasped. "That's Hensel. No wonder he dragged me into the house. I'll bet he—"

Rob held up a hand as a woman started to speak. The Queen. It took two words for me to recognize her voice. My childhood best friend and Crash's mom, Jenna Simmons.

If she and Hensel were in the meeting, where was Crash?

The radio crackled. "Shots fired."

My stomach lurched.

Then we heard, "Another body. Thirty-year-old male in a gray Impala. King of Diamonds card on his lap."

A morbid thought crept over me. The only two people unaccounted for were my dad and the Joker. "Let me out, Rob. I know who the killer is."

"Alex will send the signal," Rob said.

"Use your head, man," I shouted. "Alex is the next target! Those cards don't tell us who the person was who died but who killed them. Ian wasn't the King. My father is!"

A long ten seconds went by before Rob got out and unlocked my handcuffs. He held me back as we saw a man in costume enter the shop. Shouting for everyone to enter the building but hold their fire, Rob led the charge.

By the time I got inside, the jokers all held their hands high in the air. Rob pulled off their masks one by one like a Scooby-Doo reveal. Dog Chaney, Jenna Simmons, Franz Hensel, and Gus Allman.

Alex sighed in relief before he asked, "Where's the Joker?"

"Dead, thanks to the King," I told him, glaring at my father. "You were going to kill Alex, weren't you? The one man who was here to protect you."

My father, Gus, smirked. "How do you figure that?"

"Everyone else was accounted for. You were the only member of the gang who could've killed Joker when he arrived."

"Thankfully, there were officers nearby. And Dash," Rob added.

As I took in the sight of Gus Allman in his sequined tights and shirt, I shook my head and asked one word, "Why?"

"That's easy. I wanted to make a killing." Gus smiled, then began to laugh as officers steered him out of the building. I seriously hoped he didn't try to plead insanity, or I'd have nightmares for the rest of my life.

Who was I kidding? I would anyway.

* * *

"I'm sorry about your father," Alex said the next morning over breakfast dogs at Ricardo's food truck.

"Thanks." I set the plain dog, no bun, I ordered for my cat back in the paper bag. "He was the one who wanted me to walk the straight and narrow. I never took him for the criminal type. I even fell for his whole story about Ian orchestrating it all."

He patted my hand. "We all did, Dash."

I gazed out at the ocean with a yawn. I hadn't slept more than a couple of hours all night between phone calls from my mother and my own dark thoughts. "Did you figure out where Sophia was?"

"Hiding out with her boyfriend. She already knew Ian was dead and sure she was next."

Since my father had admitted to shooting both Ian and the Joker, some guy named Rusty O'Toole, which was likely and alias, either my father made the call to Sophia, or...

"My mother called her, didn't she?" I asked. "She knew everything."

Alex nodded, then took a bite of his dog. Egg yolk leaked down his chin.

I stared at my hot dog but didn't touch it. Although my stomach growled, the rest of me was numb. There was one other person worse off than me after this case. "What'll happen to Crash now that most of his family's dead or behind bars?"

"We've tracked down his father."

Finally, the one piece of gossip I'd been dying to hear. "For real? Who?"

He wiped his chin and sipped his coffee before grinning. "Josh Marley."

"Forensics Josh?"

"Seeing Crash at basketball practice was the only visitation Jenna and her family would allow. Hopefully, Sophia will be more lenient. I have a feeling she'll be happy to give him full custody."

"Yeah. I'm sure raising a ten-year-old boy would cramp her lifestyle," I said. "How are Crash and Josh taking things?"

Alex leaned to his right to look past me. "We'll have to ask them when they get here."

I turned to see Josh and Crash walking toward us. How had I never noticed the resemblance? They even wore matching blue hats. I smiled and knew Crash would be far better off from now on. So much for my aversion to small animals and children. This one was beginning to grow on me.

-The End-

GONE TO THE DOLLS

DIANE BATOR

ASH ALLMAN MYSTERIES BOOK 7

Gone to the Dolls

Dash Allman PI, Book 7

Diane Bator

Escape With a Writer Publishing

Did you ever have the feeling you'd been scammed but had no idea how to prove it?

My senses were tingling as my eyes narrowed. That didn't stop the scam artist—a twelve-year-old girl—from walking away with my cash leaving me with a small box of padding for my butt, aka chocolate mint cookies. Over my earbuds, Jimmy Buffett crooned about gypsies in his house while he was away.

I sighed and slammed the door pretty sure she'd charged me double for half the regular number of chocolate mint morsels. Guess she was determined to win the skateboard or bike, or whatever the current prize for the top seller was. Since I didn't like kids much, I didn't keep up with trends.

Lucky, my black cat, and I cuddled on the couch. He with his kibble treats. Me with my cookies. Between mouthfuls, I sang along with Jimmy Buffett and Alan Jackson. It was only eleven o'clock in the morning, but a girl could dream about enjoying Happy Hour somewhere tropical while scarfing down an entire box of chocolate mint cookies, couldn't she?

After the last few cases I'd dealt with, I was tired of kids, llamas, parents—especially mine—and cops. I couldn't do anything about the cat. He'd settled in and had no respect for the boundaries I'd drawn. I itched to hang a "gone fishin'" sign on my door even though I hated fishing. I also needed to pay the rent. Pro bono cases didn't cover my expenses and there was no way my parents would help out. They had enough trouble on their hands these days.

"Lucky, we need a vacation," I told him. "Too bad I don't have enough money in the bank to make it to the end of the pier."

The cat meowed, then purred and stood on his head before sliding down the back of the couch into a neat little ball.

I laid my head back and wished I could sleep so peacefully. Visions of my landlord evicting me danced in my head. I needed a well-paying gig soon, or I'd have to find a big cardboard box on the beach to sleep in.

When someone knocked on my door, I realized I'd fallen asleep and was covered in chocolate crumbs. Brushing them onto the floor, I bent over and shook my hair to get rid of any flat spots. I opened the door and was greeted by a short, round woman. As she removed her wide-framed sunglasses, I noticed her delicate fingers and the red puffiness around her bright blue eyes.

"I'm looking for Dash Allman," she said, her voice crackling with tears.

Stepping back, I expected her to hand over a restraining order or a court summons. "That's me."

"May I come in?" she asked.

I nodded, still wary. She didn't seem like the type to be selling cookies or work for the legal system. Although, I had been wrong before.

"Have a seat." I waved a hand toward the table where I normally discussed business. She settled on the far end of the couch and reached for one of my cookies. Offended by her presumption, I mumbled, "Please. Help yourself."

She paused with the chocolate cookie half inside her mouth. "Oh, dear. I'm sorry. I'm a stress eater, and right now... Oh, it's just awful."

A pang of sympathy later, I sat on the opposite end of the couch with my own cookie. "Same here. What can I do for you?"

"My name is Joy Jotty," she told me. "I'm the president of the local chapter of the Society of Miniaturists. Our members love all things dollhouse and miniature. We're having a conference at one of the downtown hotels in two weeks and I'm afraid someone has stolen my award-winning, antique dollhouse."

Lucky stretched, tapping my leg, then went back to sleep.

When I realized I was staring at her with my half-full mouth open, I narrowed my eyes. "You want me to find a dollhouse?"

"I have photographs if that helps."

"Can't you just buy a new one?"

Joy's laugh verged on hysteria, or tears. "In two weeks? Honey, the one they stole took me three years to perfect."

"Three years?" I'd never spent three years on anything except being a bad detective whose antics went viral online at every turn. My relationships all fizzled by the six-month mark. Any plant life that entered my dwelling died within a week of moving in with me. So far, the cat was faring well. Good thing he could catch rodents and bugs.

"I'll pay your going rate," she said, already munching another cookie.

Rent in mind, I jacked up my going rate by fifty bucks. I needed a new pair of flip-flops and some cat food. Oh, and more cookies.

Joy reached into her Coach handbag and took out a wad of bills. "Keep track of your expenses. I'll be happy to cover them."

My gaze fell on the cookies as she took one more. I'd add the box to my expense list. Then I counted the cash. The last time I'd seen that many bills was inside the cat lady's safe next door.

"I'll give you a bonus if you can get it back undamaged before the conference."

My heart soared. How could I say no to that? I'd never received a bonus in my life. "I'll do my best. Do you have any idea who might've stolen your doll house?"

When she pulled a manila envelope from her purse, I winced. Hopefully, she had fewer than fifty names or this would take me until Christmas.

Joy reached into the envelope and pulled out three photos. "This is my baby. She's a ten room, Victorian mansion with a working piano, gingerbread trim, and a claw-foot bathtub."

Then she handed me a photo of a thin man with little hair wearing thick glasses. "This is John Freedman. He's been a runner up for years and threatens to get even with me for winning five years running."

"Seems straightforward enough," I said as I took the photo from her.

"Hold your horses, Missy. He's only Suspect Number One."

I tried hard not to roll my eyes, but they made it halfway around.

"Suspect Number Two is Mildred Choi. She's small, but feisty. Rumor has it she has a whole new house ready to roll out for this show and won't give anyone hints. My guess is, she stole my precious dollhouse to eliminate the competition."

"Mildred. Check." I took the second photo.

Joy removed another picture from the envelope. "Suspect Number Three is Lila Dahl. Not her real name, I'm sure. She's new on the circuit and a real threat. We've all seen her videos on social media. Since I'm the one to beat, she might've taken my house to knock me out of the running early."

I scratched my head not sure when Joy began to channel a sports commentator. Did these people really take miniatures and dollhouse making that seriously?

"I wrote their names and addresses on the backs of their photos," Joy said. "There are more photos of my missing dollhouse in the envelope. Let me know what you find."

With that, Joy took one last cookie and walked out my front door.

Yikes. I guess they did. Not having a clue what I was getting into, I turned on my computer and delved into the world of miniatures. No small task. There were hundreds of websites and thousands of videos all over the internet. Everything from designing to building your dream dollhouse and all its décor and furnishings.

After a couple hours of searching for information on Joy's suspects, I was practically bug-eyed. It was time to do things the old-fashioned way.

Dash Allman was going undercover.

* * *

John Freedman opened his door, then peered out at me over the chain that created a three-inch gap. "Can I help you?"

I'd rehearsed my speech ten times while riding over on my moped over. "My name is Ash Manall. I'm a new reporter at Dollhouse Fanciers online magazine. I wondered if you had time for an interview."

The one eye I could see widened before he asked, "Are you serious, young lady? With the conference two weeks away, I barely have time to eat?"

I bowed my head and tried to look as dejected as possible. It wasn't hard. My pantyhose were creeping into parts unknown. Hence my discomfort.

"Very well," he said. "I can spare a few minutes. But you have to promise not to take any photos."

I forced a relieved smile and gushed, "Oh wonderful! Thank you so much, Mr. Freedman. I've heard a great deal about you and your work. I can't wait to learn more."

John shut the door in my face.

My mouth hanging open, I stared at the closed door in stunned surprise. A few seconds later, the chain rattled before he opened the door and ushered me inside. I was greeted by the scents of musty antiques, glue, and curry.

"I was about to have lunch," he told me. "Would you like to join me?"

So much for five minutes. I pushed my sunglasses to the top of my head. "I'd like that. It smells wonderful."

He led the way to a cozy country kitchen, complete with cows everywhere including on the doors of every oak cupboard. Black and white cows bordered the tablecloth beneath a vase adorned with a larger cow and several partly shriveled red carnations.

"I hope you're okay with chicken curry," he said. "I learned how to make it when I was a professor in Bombay. My housekeeper was a fabulous cook. In turn, I taught her all about miniatures and made dollhouses for her grandkids."

I paused to examine a bookstore diorama about nine inches tall. For a non-reader, I actually recognized a handful of author names. Hemingway. Baldacci. Shakespeare. King. Slaughter. Gazing around at his collection of cows, I asked, "Did you teach classes on miniatures at the university?"

"Actually, I teach Astrophysics," he said. "My head may be in the stars, but the miniatures keep my feet on the ground and help to keep me detail oriented."

"Makes sense."

John turned to face me. "Let me guess. Journalism major. Art History minor."

I flinched, hoping lunch didn't involve a pop quiz. "You got me."

"Let me show you something you may appreciate." He opened a door near the far end of the table.

The room had blackout curtains. For a heartbeat, I was sure I was about to be clubbed over the head and locked inside. I barely saw him reach in front of me to flick the light on. I gasped. The entire room was lined with shelves, bins, and miniature models of every kind of furniture. The dollhouse on the worktable stood three feet high with several small rooms and a metal, spiral staircase that led from an upper balcony off a large bedroom to a rooftop garden.

"Everything you see here is handmade, except the music box in the baby grand piano," he told me. "This house is my new entry in this year's show, which is why I said no photos. I've just finished a couple details. That spiral staircase is made from a wooden fan. The steamer trunk is pure balsa wood and paint. Oh, and this hot tub used to hold cheese."

When something on the stove boiled over, he retreated to the kitchen. "Pardon me."

Left unattended, I snapped a few photos for use in my case and to study later. For my case. Particularly of the rooftop garden that I would love in my backyard. My phone, in airplane mode, was tucked back into my purse by the time John returned and announced lunch was ready.

The food was delicious. We talked about everything but Joy Jotty. Until I brought up her missing dollhouse. He tensed from head to foot, including his hair, which seemed to bristle on the top of his head.

"Is that why you're here? Did that old nag tell you I stole her decrepit old house?"

Wide-eyed, I shook my head. "No. I heard about the theft from some other aficionados."

"Now look what you've done," John said. "You've made my hands shake. Now I won't get any work done this afternoon. Perhaps you should leave."

"I could help you with the dishes."

"I'll do them. It relaxes me."

Standing, I prepared to let him show me out. When my host didn't move, I retreated to the front entrance, closing the door behind me. I was surprised he never asked to see my phone in case I might be a traitor. Which I was.

What I wouldn't give for a chocolate mint cookie.

* * *

Mildred Choi was next on Joy's list. After John's reaction when I mentioned Joy, I wanted to wait for my indigestion to settle down before facing another suspect.

I grabbed a soda from Ricardo's food truck on the beach near my house and put in my ear buds while I sat in the sand to clear my head. Jimmy Buffett sang about attitudes and latitudes. Boy, could I use a change in both. When the next song came on about pirates, my thoughts drifted to the photo of Joy's missing dollhouse.

The picture she showed me was far less detailed and elaborate than John's design. His was a brand-new creation, which might have something to do with upping his game. I doubted it would take much to surpass Joy's house in competition. From what I'd seen, he had no reason to steal hers.

Mildred's home was within walking distance, so I strolled along a few side streets until I reached her cottage and knocked on the bright blue door. She was a frail, gray-haired, blue-eyed woman who stood a stooped six inches shorter than me. She appeared twenty years older than in the photo Joy gave me.

I recited my speech about being Ash Manall working for the magazine before she coughed and motioned for me to follow her inside. Cringing as her chest rattled and wheezed, I had serious doubts she had anything to do with the theft. She could barely walk or breathe let alone carry a three-foot tall doll house.

"Joy Jotty sent you, didn't she?" Mildred gasped, reaching for an oxygen mask as she sat on a faded blue recliner.

I gave up the charade and wondered why Joy hadn't mentioned Mildred was ill. "Yes."

She pulled the mask away long enough to flash a grin. "I assume she showed you photos of her missing dollhouse. That monstrosity's ready for mothballs. Just like her."

Uninvited, I sat on a nearby chair, so I could hear better. "I take it you think she should stop competing."

"More like she should stop living in the past. Build a new house and move on. John's going to win this year anyway."

"Have you seen his house?" I asked.

"Only the pictures he showed me," she said, pausing to cough, then wiped her mouth with a tissue.

A shudder snaked down my back. I never wanted to be in her position. "I take it you're not competing this year."

Mildred took as deep a breath from the mask as she could, then shook her head. "Too busy dying."

"I'm sorry to hear that."

She shrugged. "That's life. I'm not going anywhere until I see Joy lose."

"I take it you two have a pretty intense rivalry," I said.

"Since kindergarten. Seventy years."

I whistled. "That's a long time to hold a grudge."

"Right?" Mildred took another deep breath from the mask. "Joy always wants to be the best. You want to see my work room, don't you?"

After seeing John's fantastic space and his doll house, I was intrigued. "I'd love to."

"Don't worry," she said. "I'm not a stickler like John. You can take all the pictures you want. In fact, you can take whichever house you want. What do I need them for?" As I stood, she reached out a hand. "Help me up?"

Once on her feet, she leaned against me to get to the next room, then asked me to turn on the light. Just like at John's house, the entire room was lined with shelves filled with dioramas. Bookstores, coffee shops, campers, a beach house, even the North Pole complete with a sleeping Santa in front of a fireplace. The one that caught my eye was an elaborate garden behind what looked like a stone castle.

"Holy crackers," I whispered, helping her ease onto a stool before flitting from one piece of art to the next for closer looks.

"Pick your favorite," she said, her voice raspy. "My gift."

I gazed around the room at the hundred plus dioramas. It would take hours just to look at them all. How was I supposed to choose one?

"Does Joy think I stole her dollhouse?" she asked. "Don't look so surprised, Dash. I see you on the news regularly."

My cheeks burned. So much for undercover work. "Joy gave me a list. You, John, and Lila Dahl."

Mildred cleared her throat, then asked, "Do I look capable of stealing something that size and getting away unnoticed?"

I took the other chair near her worktable and gazed at lamps, perfume bottles, and vases made from assorted beads and bead caps. Tiny candles sat on one-inch mirror trays. "Did you make all these?"

"I did. My passion for the past forty years since my kids all left home. I couldn't bear to part with the dollhouse my father made when I was little, so I repaired it. Once I won my first contest with it, the bug took hold. I've created hundreds of them since." Her face glowed as she spoke. She hadn't gasped for breath at all since we'd entered the craft room.

"They're incredible," I told her. "You're very talented."

Her pale cheeks crinkled as she smiled. "You can't decide, can you?"

I shook my head.

"I might know just the right one," she said. "That wall. Fourth shelf down. Sixth house from the far end."

Following her instructions, I found a tiny beach house with tropical, floral-patterned furniture, a lanai off the back room filled with plants and a chair swing, and a pet bed that held a black cat and a llama. I burst into laughter.

"I couldn't resist," Mildred said. "I added the animals after John called."

"He knew who I was?" I asked, meeting her gaze.

She chuckled. "John watches the news too, love. He enjoyed watching you squirm before you left, but felt bad for toying with you."

Picking up the miniature beach house, I asked, "Who else did he tell?"

"Just me. He doesn't trust anyone else, especially Joy or Lila."

"How come?" I returned to the chair and shook my head as I gazed at the cat and the llama once more.

"Past experience," she said, then proceeded to show me a couple tricks for making candles using straws of various widths. After that, we moved on to crafting bottles made from beads.

Right after I managed to get the glue off my fingers, my phone rang. Unknown number. That wasn't unusual in my line of work. I let it go to voicemail.

"Would you be a dear and help me to the sofa, Dash?" Mildred asked. "I need a nap. I don't usually have this much excitement in the afternoon."

"Of course."

I helped her get settled, then fetched her a glass of water and a blanket. As I left with my baby beach house, I locked the door behind me as instructed. The entire six blocks home, I tried to decide where to put it, so Lucky wouldn't knock it on the floor.

That's when it hit me. I understood about the llama, but how did Mildred know I had a black cat?

***

Turned out the call I'd missed was from Joy, who demanded an update. She'd have to wait. I still couldn't explain how Mildred knew about Lucky. My only guess was that Joy told her, but when? If they were such sworn enemies, why would Joy speak to her?

I set the diorama on my table to take a closer look. Llama. Black cat. Plants that weren't dead. The chair swing. When I focused on the pictures on the wall, a shiver ran down my neck and ended at my tailbone.

Every photo was of me. Ones that a stalker or private investigator would take.

I called Rob Gwynn, my most recent on and off boyfriend, who was on the police force. No answer. Apparently, we'd been "off" for months. He never even told me when he was going on leave for back surgery or where he'd been since.

My next call was to his partner, Alex Carson who seemed determined to retire before I got him killed. His answer fit our decades long friendship. "What are you into now, Dash?"

"Hello to you, too," I replied. "Do you know a woman named Mildred Choi? She's—"

"Funny you should ask," he said. "We got a robbery call to Mildred's house half an hour ago and found her dead on the couch. The caller said they recognized the lady from the llama video leaving the scene with one of Mildred's dollhouses."

Oh, great. I closed my eyes. "Can I call you right back?"

"Depends. Where are you?" he asked.

"My place. With said dollhouse. It's a beach house she gave me before I helped her get settled for a nap on her couch."

"You sure you didn't put a pillow over her face while you were at it?"

"Pretty sure."

Alex sighed. "Okay. I had to ask. Don't leave. I'll be right over."

"I'm broke. Where am I gonna go?"

Hanging up, I returned my attention to the mini beach house. My gut told me Mildred had left me more than just a few stalker photos. Had she and John teamed up to steal Joy's dollhouse together?

I doubted it. Besides, I still needed to talk to Lila Dahl. And to Joy Jotty, who was next on my list. Since I couldn't leave my house without Alex arresting me, I returned Joy's call.

"Where have you been?" she asked, her voice shrill.

"Talking to your suspects."

There was a silence at the other end while Lucky yawned and stretched beside me, then leaped from the couch and padded to the table.

"What have you found?" she asked.

"Not much, but I still need to talk to one more person."

"Who?"

When I glanced at the dollhouse, something nudged me to tell her, "Mildred."

A long silence followed. Did she know I was lying? If she said anything about Mildred's death, I'd know the whole case was a fraud. Finally, she said, "Okay. Call me when you know anything."

Considering I mostly flew by the seat of my pants, I doubted I'd have any reason to call her before the end of the day. Especially with Alex on his way over and a set of shiny handcuffs looming in my future.

Those pictures on the wall of the tiny beach house bothered me. I snapped a shot of them, then printed it so I could show the police. While I stared at them, Lucky nosed at the small armchair closest to him.

"It's furniture," I told him, stroking his head. "You can't eat it."

The cat growled before launching a full out attack on the fake rattan just as someone knocked at the front door. Unable to pry the material from Lucky's mouth, I carried him across the room to open the door. Razor claws dug into my arm as I let Alex in with a shriek. Before the burly officer could ask, Lucky dropped the miniature chair. I dropped Lucky and snatched it off the floor before he could clamp his jaws on it. Feline teeth sank into my index finger and drew blood.

By the time Lucky, the chair, and I all went our separate ways, Alex sat on the couch with tears streaming down his red face.

"Seriously?" I asked, clutching my finger while Lucky strolled to his water bowl.

"You know, I used to dread coming to any call within a ten-mile radius of you," Alex told me. "Now I kind of look forward to them for this reason. Too bad this one won't go viral. It watch it over and over."

I picked up the chair and sat at the far end of the couch. "Thanks for your concern."

"You'd better get that finger looked at. You don't want it to get infected."

"Tell me what you know about Mildred." I scowled before hugging a couch cushion and taking a closer look at the gash in my finger.

He shook his head. "Not until you tell me why you went to see her."

"We're old friends. We go way back."

"To this morning, I'm sure. Try again."

I filled him in on Joy Jotty's visit, my chat with John, then my stop at Mildred's house. "She gave me the doll house. Complete with a llama and a black cat."

"I see." He took the little chair and looked it over before he asked, "Why were you and Lucky fighting over this?"

"He stole it from the beach house. She probably stuffed the cushions with catnip or something." I motioned him over to the table and handed him the photo I'd printed. "This is a close up of the photos on the wall."

As Alex looked at the miniature photos of me at the beach, me at the market, and me at Ricardo's eating a breakfast dog, his frown etched deeper. "Was she stalking you?"

"Someone was. I'm starting to have a bad feeling about Joy Jotty. I don't suppose you can check her out for me, could you?"

"And what are you going to do?"

"For now? Put the beach house in the cupboard to keep it away from Catzilla, then go talk to Lila Dahl." I showed him the photos Joy gave me.

"Just be careful, will you?"

I scoffed. "I'm always careful."

Alex looked at my bloody finger. "Yeah. Right."

Once he left, I had a hunch. I carefully picked apart the cushion on the little chair. Inside the seat was a small vial filled with tiny rocks. Whatever it was, Mildred gave it to me for a reason. Now I just had to figure out what that was and what to do about it.

* * *

Lila Dahl towered over me by nearly a foot and made Malibu Barbie look pasty. She could've been a suntan oil model. Her tight shorts and tank top left little to anyone's imagination. Alex would be disappointed he hadn't tagged along this time.

"It's about time you showed up, honey," she said in a sultry voice before I could recite my cover story.

"Excuse me?"

She scowled. "You are the detective Joy hired, aren't you?"

My shoulders dropped. "Yes."

"Good. Get in here. We need to talk." Lila didn't walk. She sashayed as though parading down a Paris runway. I imagined she left people drooling as she passed.

She led me to a sunroom at the back of her home that served as a workshop. Far from a dark, private space sealed off from the world, this room was wide open and bright. "I hope you don't mind if I work while we chat. I only have a couple weeks until the judges' preview."

Preview? That was something no one had mentioned.

"You look confused. Let me guess, no one mentioned preview night."

"No, they didn't."

Lila's snort surprised me. "Joy must assume she'll have her house ready by then."

"Didn't you hear? Her dollhouse was stolen."

"Sure, it was." She laughed. "Her security alarm doesn't even let her husband in the house without her assistance. How could someone get inside to steal her ugly old dollhouse?"

"That's interesting."

She shrugged as she sat in front of a six-inch wide magnifying glass on an extendable arm. "I might be exaggerating, but the odds of anyone stealing that three-story monstrosity are thin to zilch, honey. It's as out of date as she is."

I claimed a nearby stool and watched in silence as she created a tiny envelope using tweezers and a thin ruler, then added a cute sticker to the back to seal it. "That's impressive. I could never do what you do. I'm not that creative."

"And I couldn't solve a mystery if one bit me on the nose," she said. "Do you have any questions for me, or should I teach you a few tricks of the trade?"

Laughing, I told her about nearly gluing my fingers together at Mildred's house. "I'll pass. I do have one off topic question for you. What would make a cat want to eat a particular piece of dollhouse furniture?"

"Starvation or catnip," she replied. "My cats hate the smell of the glues, so my pieces are safe. I suppose it depends what kind of glue or fabric the person used."

I'd have to check the beat-up chair later and ask Alex if they could find out what kind of glue Mildred used. Pointing to Lila's two-story, Tudor-style structure, I asked, "Is this the house you're entering in the contest?"

Lila grinned. "This is my red herring. I'm keeping the real one hidden until the preview. Since I know you've seen John and Mildred's houses, I'll trust you."

My stomach rolled. "You don't know."

"Don't know what?" She set down the tweezers.

"Mildred passed away. The police got a call about an hour ago."

When Lila dropped her glue, it landed on the tiny envelope. "Aunt Mildred's dead?"

"Mildred was your aunt?"

"Actually, she was my ex-husband's aunt. I left him, but I kept her in the divorce. Mildred taught me everything I know."

I got off my stool. "I'm sorry for your loss. Maybe I should give you some privacy."

"Please stay." She grabbed my hand. "I'll make Zumbani tea. It's good for everything, including grief. I just don't want to be alone right now."

The tea was lemony, and I savored it while Lila showed me pictures on her computer of past dollhouse conferences she'd attended with Mildred. Joy was present at every one of them. While Joy wore a huge smile, her gaze was usually slanted toward Mildred or Lila.

"Could you send me some of the pictures with both Mildred and Joy?" I asked.

"What do you see?"

I shook my head. "Maybe it's nothing. Were they always such rivals?"

"Joy insisted there was a rivalry," she said. "Mildred and the rest of us go to events to make new friends and learn new skills. We're like family."

If they were anything like my family, there'd be a snake or two among them happy to steal the competition's entry. "How long have you been divorced?"

"Six months. I inherited the house from my mom, and the cars were in my name. I gave him one car and the downtown apartment. Other than that, I cut the gold digger off."

My nose twitched smelling a motive. "Would you mind if I talked to him? He might know who'd want to hurt his aunt."

"I doubt it, but feel free. If you can get a word in edgewise." Lila searched a drawer in the build-in bookcase, then handed me a card. "Just don't expect him to say anything nice, especially me. As far as he's concerned, we're all geeks and mutants."

As I walked back to my moped, I realized I never saw her entry for the contest. Was that intentional on her part or was she side-tracked by word of Mildred's death?

* * *

Before I even knocked on Geoff Wilson's door, I heard him all the way down the street. The door opened to reveal Lila Dahl's ex-husband, who was six-foot-ten, built like a telephone pole, and spoke louder than a broken air-conditioner when he growled, "Whaddya want?"

"Hi, I'm Ash Manall," I began.

My speech was interrupted by two boys fighting behind him. "I want it." "I want it." They went back and forth until Geoff stepped between them and grabbed the ball.

"It's mine and you can't have it," he shouted. "Go find the cookies. The ice cream truck'll be here soon."

Once the boys ran off, he turned back to me and repeated, "Whaddya want?"

The sheer volume of his voice made me take an uncomfortable step back. My mind went blank.

"Let me guess," he barked. "Lila sent you. Tell her there's no way I'll take her back. Ever. She's not enough woman for me. Real women don't play with dollhouses."

Before I could reply, he slammed the door in my face. The familiar tune of the ice cream truck echoed through the quiet street as I wiped his spittle off my face. I'd rather deal with the llama. I ducked into the bushes near his fence before he and the boys stampeded past me and down the street.

Since they'd left the door wide open, I snuck into the house.

Trespassing? Technically, but I had no desire to speak to that man again if I didn't have to. With no idea how much time I had I kept my senses on high alert as I darted from one room to the next looking for Joy's dollhouse. Any other items that seemed out of place would do. That was why the sight of broken, miniature furniture stopped my search.

I took photos of the beads, stuffing, and what looked like miniature cutlery, then scooped a couple pieces into a bag in my purse. With any luck, Geoff wouldn't notice them missing. Although my luck was anything but good most days.

I darted out the screen door in back just as Geoff's voice boomed from the front sidewalk. The dog and I both growled, then locked gazes. I wasn't willing to hop another fence. Last time, I'd tore my dress and nearly flashed news crews. I ducked and ran toward the side of the house with the rottweiler in hot pursuit.

"Please don't bite me," I whispered. My heart hammered as I reached for the latch on the side gate and flicked it open. Before I could make a hasty escape, the dog barreled past me and down the street to freedom. "I didn't expect that."

As Geoff's front door opened, I ran up his neighbor's front steps and pretended to ring the bell as if making rounds of the neighborhood.

"Hey," he yelled.

I froze, not daring to move.

"You see a black dog run by? My lazy nephews forgot to lock the gate."

I pointed up the street. While Geoff lumbered after the dog, I raced in the opposite direction toward my moped. I'd send the pictures of the broken furniture to Alex once I got home. I'd also call Joy to see if she knew Geoff.

Right after I locked all my doors and windows, my heart rate slowed to normal, and I could breathe again.

* * *

Alex's first question when I texted the photos was, *"Did he invite you inside?"*

"I'm not a vampire," I replied.

"Dash."

"His door was open. I was looking for him after talking to another suspect."

Not the complete truth but close enough.

"I'll see what I can do," he told me.

Joy's response when I asked about Geoff was filled with expletives loud enough to make Lucky hide under the bed. I wondered if the two of them were related before she snarled, "Who told you about that rat?"

"Lila."

Silence.

"Joy?" I asked.

A heavy sigh. "I'll be right over. You need to hear this in person. Someone might be listening to us."

I threw the last of my chocolate mint cookies into the freezer.

Joy Jotty was on my doorstep in less than ten minutes. She came bearing three large milkshakes from Ricardo's food truck and handed me one. "I needed comfort food."

Chocolate mint. For a split second, I felt bad about hiding the cookies. That passed with the next sip as she slurped one of the other shakes. When we sat on the couch, Lucky appeared out of nowhere to create a short, furry fence between us.

"Geoff Wilson is a...," she started, then paused. "Never mind. You heard that part."

"I take it you know him through Lila."

Joy grimaced. "Other way around. I know Lila through Geoff. He's my baby brother. My whole life, that boy's been a thorn in my backside. When our parents died, he got worse. Our older brother was our legal guardian who had to work two jobs to look after us. I started babysitting when I was fourteen, which left Geoff alone some nights. Not our best decision. He was nine and constantly in trouble. Paulie lost one job after Geoff and a buddy stole beer from the gas station he worked at."

"When he was nine?" I asked.

She sucked on her straw, which made a loud gurgle, then switched to the extra milkshake. "Oh, no. He was ten by then."

I closed my eyes and shook my head. My parents thought I was an out-of-control kid. I was nothing compared to Geoff Wilson.

"He's been in and out of trouble since we were little," she continued. "Geoff fell off the roof one night while peeping at the neighbor's daughter. Our parents were taking him to the hospital when they went off the road and crashed into a tree. He walked home on a broken leg and went to bed without saying a word. Paulie and I had no idea what happened until the police came to tell us they were dead. Last I heard, he was selling drugs."

Geoff Wilson was beginning to scare me even more.

"Did you ever find out what happened to your parents that night?" I asked.

"Nope," she said, then went back to work on her milkshake. Her cheeks caved in on either side of her straw.

With a gut feeling she knew more than she was willing to tell me, I placed the pieces of doll furniture on the coffee table. "Do these look familiar?"

"They belong to Mildred."

"Your aunt."

"Who told you that?" she asked, then went on. "Lila. Never mind. Someone stole that set at a show a few months ago. Did Geoff have them?"

"Yes."

"Strange I never saw him at any of the shows. That must've been before Lila broke up with him and he met that new floozy. Jen or Gwen. Something like that."

Joy set down the milkshake and pulled out her phone to show me half a dozen photos of her dollhouse and her suspects. One of the photos showed Lila and Mildred in front of a large, gothic dollhouse. Instead of gingerbread trim, it had something that looked like black spider webs. Lila held up a white ribbon.

"Whose house is that?" I asked.

"Lila's original one before she remodeled it. Good thing she did. That one was hideous."

I stifled a chuckle. The judges didn't seem to agree with her since Lila took third place. "Remodeled it how?"

Joy swiped to another photo showing a pastel, Victorian mansion with the same gingerbread trim but vastly different finishings. Even though the first image looked like something the Addams family would love, the sudden change from gothic to the Victorian mansion bothered me. I asked Joy to forward the photos, so I could take a closer look.

"Why did she make such a major change to her entry?"

"No idea. It was a good move, if you ask me." Once she'd sent the photos, she reached for her drink. This time, her hand shook.

Lucky also seemed to notice her sudden attack of nerves and inched toward me.

"Do you think Geoff had something to do with that?" I asked.

Joy nodded. "Possibly, or..."

"Or?"

She sent me one more photo and told me to look at the figure in blue who had a camera strap around her neck. "Her name is Gwen. Gwendolyn Mayer. She's a newbie. The floozy Geoff was flirting with. We've all given her advice when she asked and were more than generous. It's just that she's kind of odd."

"Odd how?" I asked.

"Quiet. Dark. She loved Lila's gothic house so much that she tried to buy it several times, but Lila refused."

"Is that why she changed it?"

Joy's voice grew much quieter when she said, "I couldn't tell you. All I know is they had an awful argument in the parking lot after that last show."

She not only had photos of the argument, but some showing Lila leaning toward the shorter Gwendolyn menacingly. She also had Gwendolyn's address and a major stomachache after sucking back two milkshakes. Much to my relief, she went home to find some antacids.

I decided to do a little web surfing before calling Alex. "Hey, I need to ask a big favor."

"How do you keep getting into these things?" he asked, before I could go on.

"What do you mean?"

"We have another body."

A little voice inside me whispered, *"Please be Geoff."* In my grown-up voice, I asked, "Who is it?"

"Lila Dahl."

"Lila?" I swallowed hard. The room seemed to spin around me, but I was sure it was because of all the sugar I'd consumed. I needed real food. Like a breakfast dog. "I'll be right over. I need to check on something."

"Dash, I don't—," he started.

I hung up before he could finish. After feeding Lucky, I grabbed the broken pieces of dollhouse furniture and my phone, then ran over to Lila's house. Alex and Rob met me at the front gate, blocking my path.

"You really don't want to go in there," Alex said.

My legs quivered. The last time I ran was at Christmas behind the llama, which hardly counted. He'd done all the running. I'd just hung on for dear life. "No, I don't. But I have to."

He shook his head. "Trust me, Dash. Not this time."

I turned to Rob. "What if I promise to close my eyes until we get to the craft room?"

"That's where the body is," Rob said.

Frustrated, I placed my hands on my hips with my fingers crossed as best I could. "You know I'll find a way inside. I was here earlier today and can tell you if something's missing."

They relented. Giving me booties, a hairnet, and gloves, they led me inside—Alex walked in front and Rob behind me to make sure I didn't touch anything. The first thing I noticed when we stepped into Lila's brightly lit workroom was that someone had torn apart dozens of pieces of carefully constructed doll house furniture.

The second, was that the body on the tile floor wasn't Lila Dahl. This woman was shorter, softer, and bloodier. Since there was only one person on my radar that I hadn't met yet, I took a wild guess. "According to Joy, that's Gwendolyn Mayer."

All eyes in the room, police and forensics, turned toward me.

"You'd better be one hundred percent positive," Rob said.

I wasn't, but I stuck to my story. "I need a closer look at the piece Lila was working on."

Rob huffed. "Why?"

Josh Marley, one of the forensics techs stepped aside while keeping a close eye on me. We'd met on the Cat Lady case and bumped into each other a few times since. Josh rolled his eyes, then asked, "What are you looking for?"

"A clue. Like these." I pointed to a couple crumbs on the table.

"What do cookie crumbs prove?" Alex asked.

"Nothing on their own." I told them about finding the vial in the mini chair from Mildred and how she'd insisted I take the little beach house, complete with llama and a black cat like Lucky.

"You should've given the vial to Alex," Josh said. "Whatever's in there could be dangerous."

I raised my eyebrows. "How dangerous?"

"Big time drug dangerous."

Taking a deep breath, I turned back to the dollhouse and began to press on beds, sofas, and chair seats with my gloved fingers. I asked Josh for markers and put one on each hard spot. After he took photos of each piece of furniture, he used a knife to slice one open. Sure enough, there was another tiny vial. I gazed around us at the dozens of dioramas and dollhouses. Every one of them had places vials could be hidden. All had tags with various letters.

"Are you trying to tell us Lila Dahl was hiding drugs in the doll-houses?" Alex shook his head. "That's a first for me."

My mouth went dry. "I don't think it was just Lila. The one I found was in the one Mildred gave me."

Rob looked around the room. "I'll bet those tags have codes to say which drugs are hidden inside. I think we've stumbled onto something bigger than a murder here."

Josh pointed to the doorway. "You guys need to leave. We'll package everything and take it all back to the lab. You may want to call drug enforcement on your way out."

Alex glanced toward the vial in Josh's hand. "You think our suspects have an operation somewhere in town?"

"Wait what?" I asked.

Josh threw an arm around my shoulders. "Congratulations, Dash Allman, you may have just helped the police bust a nefarious drug ring."

"But these people decorate dollhouses. They all seemed so nice," I told them, then gazed down at Gwendolyn. A high-end camera lay a foot away from her bloody hand. "I take that back."

"Did you walk here?" Alex asked.

"Ran. My legs hurt."

"We'll drop you off at home," Rob said, taking my arm to walk me to the front door.

I stopped between them, remembering the last clue. "Not yet. I know who killed Gwendolyn, and maybe Mildred."

"You do?" Josh asked, raising his eyebrows.

As Alex hustled me out of the room, I yelled, "Bag those cookie crumbs!"

Once we got to the car, Alex stuffed me into the back seat. He and Rob sat in the front with their doors closed and locked and the engine running before he asked, "Where are we going?"

Thinking fast, I gave him John Freedman's address.

We pulled up just as a red car parked in his driveway. Joy Jotty stormed up the sidewalk wearing capris and a dark hoodie. She seemed oblivious to the squad car.

"That's Joy Jotty. Darn. She beat us here." I reached for the door handle, then remembered where I was. "You need to let me out."

"You're staying put," Rob growled.

He and Alex ran to the front door and drew their weapons. Joy was already inside. I closed my eyes and feared for everyone's safety. A minute later, I ran out of patience.

"Oh, come on!" I shouted, bouncing on the back of the car. "You could've at least left a window cracked or the air conditioning on. It's bloody hot in here."

Just as beads of sweat seeped from my forehead, the two officers walked out with Joy, John, and Lila in front of them. Rob opened the back door to my left and ordered all three to get in.

"Are you serious?" I shrieked.

"This is highly unorthodox," John announced. "I demand an explanation."

Joy scooted across the seat, then squished me against the door and barked, "I demand you tell us why we're being detained." Lila and John were wedged against the other door.

"Can we get some air back here?" Lila asked. "I'm going to faint."

I couldn't move and gasped. "Same here."

Couldn't breathe.

Couldn't speak. Although, I didn't have to. John and Joy said more than enough for all of us as they argued over top of Lila.

Joy tried to move her right arm, presumably to punch John, but was stuck. Something hard dug into my left ribs.

"You can breathe when we get to the station," Alex told them. "In fact, you can tell us everything about Mildred Choi and Gwendolyn Mayer's murders on the way."

"Gwen's dead?" Lila asked. She passed out on top of Joy, who shoved her onto John.

The poor man seemed to have no idea what to do or where to put his hands. Finally, he said, "Let me out of this municipal clown mobile and I'll tell you whatever you want to know. Just get Lila some medical help. She's ill."

"From the meth lab?" I asked.

It was a wild jab in the dark that seemed to hit home. Everyone in the car fell silent for several seconds before Joy growled.

"You told her," she said.

"I swear, I never said a word." John shook his head, which was the only thing he could move with Lila on top of him.

Joy tried to move her right arm again and knocked what little wind I still had right out of me. "All I wanted was my fair share from our little endeavor. If the rest of you hadn't shut me out of the trade, none of this would've happened."

John's face—well, the cheek I could see past Joy's head—turned red. "Yeah? Well, if you hadn't killed Millie and Gwen, we'd still be in operation and making wads of money."

Both suddenly seemed to remember they were in the back seat of a police car.

I chuckled. "Not one of your finest forms of interrogation, boys, but still effective. Now can I go home?"

"Nope," Alex and Rob chorused.

Getting us all into the backseat was tough enough. Extracting all four of us required extra officers and a wheelchair for Lila, who went straight into the station to be assessed. An ambulance took her to hospital handcuffed to the gurney. Joy resented being searched, even when police turned up a gun and several small vials of drugs. John sat handcuffed in a hard plastic chair looking resigned to spending the rest of his life in prison.

I got a ride home in the backseat of an air-conditioned police car.

Blissfully alone and with my arms spread out on either side of me.

* * *

Josh texted me after his shift that night to let me know every miniature house held one to five vials. The combined street value was well into six figures and counting. I'd get a finder's fee for my help in busting the ring and be able to pay my rent. They'd recovered Joy's "missing" dollhouse, in a large box in her garage completely whole and with a fresh coat of paint. As well as a few small vials in the furniture.

A couple hours later, he came by to take me for a midnight stroll, which ended with a picnic on the beach. Sparkling water, crackers, cheeses, and deli meats by a bonfire was something I could get used to. We chatted about dollhouses, the strange case, and the meth lab drug enforcement discovered in the police search of Mildred's property.

"It's no wonder she was so sick," I told him, then sighed. "I never would've guessed they were all part of it."

"Yet you nailed them. What did Joy have against the others that she got you involved in their operation?" Josh asked.

"Mildred was dying and planned to hand off control of the operation to Lila. Since Joy had seniority, she fought it. The others sided with Mildred and threatened to shove Joy off the gravy train. She decided to get even by bringing a fake theft case to me instead of getting mad."

"Wow." He popped an olive into his mouth.

"That's not the worst of it. She ate half of my chocolate mint cookies."

Josh gasped. "The nerve of that woman."

I laughed, nudging his shoulder with mine.

"Good thing I came prepared," he said, taking a box of chocolate mint cookies from the picnic bag.

"How did you know?"

"I didn't. I was guilted into buying six boxes from the kids on my team. I packed two more in the bag that you can take home. I already gave one to Rob for his wife."

My sense of humor curled away with the smoke as I stared at him. "His wife?"

"Yeah. Ginny's four months pregnant and...," Josh closed his eyes before adding, "You had no idea he got married at Christmas, did you?"

Tears burned my eyes. "No wonder the creep ghosted me."

Josh draped one arm around my shoulders and rested his head against mine. "If it's any consolation, you still have me to hang out with. Unless you don't think we should be seen in public together."

"Only if you don't mind me hanging out with llamas and going viral now and then."

He laughed. "I could live with it that. You already made me famous with the kids at the community center when they found out we were friends."

I slipped my arms around his waist and buried my face in his shirt. He smelled of soap and citrus. Even after a day of bodies and crime solving.

"Mmm. Your hair smells like coconut," he murmured.

Pulling away, I gazed into his eyes. "Do you like cats?"

"Most of them. Your cat scares the crap out of me, but I'm sure a few bags of treats would help him warm up to me."

"That's the one thing Lucky and I have in common," I told him. "You feed us and we're all good. I mean, you brought cookies, and here we are."

"Yeah. Here we are," he whispered.

We kissed in the firelight before I could second guess myself. My stomach sank like I'd hit the down button in an elevator. Maybe I'd ask Alex to do a background check on Josh.

Just to be on the safe side.

Tomorrow.

-The End-

About the Author

Diane Bator began writing as a kid when she fell in love with storytelling. After ten years with various traditional publishers, she's created her own company, Escape With a Writer Publishing to relaunch her previous work plus many new titles. She is also a member of Sisters in Crime, Crime Writers of Canada, The Writers Union of Canada, and International Thriller Writers.

A proud mom of three, Diane loves a good joke. She's also a Reiki Master, a blue belt in goju-ryu karate, and an artist who loves stopping at odd places on road trips and creating new things from old.

Her website is https://dianebator.ca/

Join her newsletter and Escape With a Writer! https://dianebator.substack.com/

Also from Diane Bator

PUBLISHED BY ESCAPE WITH A WRITER PUBLISHING

Written in Stone, A.J. Cadell Mystery, Book 1
All That Sparkles, Glitter Bay Mystery, Book 1
Death of a Jaded Samurai, Gilda Wright Mystery, Book 1

Milton Keynes UK
Ingram Content Group UK Ltd.
UKHW030952261124
451585UK00001B/34